Hakujin

A NOVEL BY

Hélène Gabel Ryan

Anthes Press
P. O. Box 31521
Seattle, Washington 98103-1521

Cover photograph courtesy of Hélène Gabel Ryan

Library of Congress Control Number: 2005909505
ISBN-10: 0-9774885-0-0
ISBN-13: 978-0-9774885-0-6
SAN: 257 - 7445

Manufactured in the United States of America
Cover and text design by Gorham Printing

I

saw

the little old

Japanese lady

with

the

birdcage

on

Yesler Way

in

Seattle

one

April

day

in

1942

Preface

My grandfather came to the United States when he was fourteen in search of adventure and escape from the Kaiser's army. He settled on Puget Sound in 1880 on Whidbey Island when the southern portion was sparsely inhabited. It was paradise, he told me. Deer paused at his cabin door and he scooped salmon from nearby streams with his bare hands. According to family legend, he traveled by rowboat from the island to Seattle to attend lectures by Mark Twain, Eugene V. Debs, Robert Ingersoll, and other freethinkers like himself. Grandpa was handsome and charismatic. I adored him. I was lucky that he lived for 21 years of my life.

When I was thirteen, I began reading Grandpa's books. We were in the middle of the Big Depression. Prejudice was rampant, people told ugly jokes about other religions and ethnic backgrounds, and all nationalities had dreadful nicknames. There were no laws to protect minorities and it was a crime in some states to marry a person of another race.

I saw Japanese Americans carted away in Army trucks during the fifth month of our involvement in World War II, children and old people bound for inadequate housing in faraway places. I always believed that it wasn't just fear and prejudice that influenced the government to force 120,000 of our Japanese into exile. It was greed on the part of those who profited from the misfortunes of the evacuees.

The war was catalyst for tremendous change. The entry of women into the labor market was the most important economic and sociological event of the twentieth century. My generation of women was first in history to become an integral part of the work force. At last women could be financially independent. We were in demand during the war, but when it ended, we were expected to return home where we belonged. Many didn't. Those of us who raised baby boomers went back to work after our children were grown.

It is gratifying to look back on a long life and realize how much has been accomplished. We didn't abolish war and poverty as many hoped, but we demonstrated our feelings at times and with good results. I am glad we picketed City Hall when the Mayor and all the members of the Seattle City Council wanted to replace the Pike Place Market with a posh hotel. I am proud to have participated in the huge demonstration against the Vietnam War when we marched up Fifth Avenue, wall to wall, on our way to the Federal Building. That would have pleased my grandfather.

H. G. R.
Second edition
Spring, 2007

Acknowledgments

Heartfelt thanks for their inspiration, encouragement and enthusiasm to Ellen Davies Hale, Dayana Jon Patterson, and Gerald Elfendahl.

Photo Credits

The faces that appear in Robin's Album and on the cover of Hakujin are those of real people who represent fictional characters in a book that is fiction.

Credit is given to Seattle's Museum of History and Industry for use of Photo #20857, Post-Intelligencer Collection (Girl on Ferry), page 90; and Kitsap County Historical Society, Photo #39, Perrine Collection (Old Auto on Indianola Dock), page 91. Also used are photos from Garfield High School's 1935 yearbook, The Arrow, and photos from the author's collection.

1

Kiko and I grew up during the Great Depression and were blasted into adulthood by a world war.

We had lived peacefully, only vaguely aware that some people stared at us a lot. Now, with the war, they glared at us and projected the feeling that we had no business being chums because I am a Hakujin, a white person, and she is Japanese.

Kiko lived on Yesler Way on a hill above downtown Seattle, only a few blocks from Chinatown, and I lived on the opposite end of the same street on another hill overlooking Lake Washington. Garfield High was midway between our houses.

After school we walked up 23rd Avenue to the library where we sat on a curb with our feet in the gutter, lingering for as long as we dared. Already we had spent most of the day together with the same classes, study hall, and lunch period. But that wasn't enough.

"Robin, it's your turn to walk me home," Kiko would say hopefully after checking her watch, and I'd say, "I can't. It's getting dark already."

Disgruntled, Kiko would flounce off without so much as a wave or a goodbye.

We weren't known as teenagers in those days; we were adolescents. Even at eighteen years of age, we were absolute greenhorns. We had no television to wise us up about the ways of the world.

Kiko was shy and noncommittal, invisible in a crowd, but when we were alone together and out of earshot of everyone, her eyes flashed in anger or sparkled with pleasure as she engaged in a dress rehearsal for the day when she'd become the person she wanted to be. I thought it was neat to witness that transformation.

My mother never invited Kiko to stay overnight. I think Mom was afraid of saying or doing something embarrassing, not having had any experience with people of other races. But she did allow me to spend the night with Kiko occasionally. That's how it happened that I was with the Nakayamas the day the war broke out.

I woke up that Sunday morning in the unfinished attic, bedroom for Kiko and her younger sister, Yuki. Fanciful ice etchings on the inside panes of the windows had begun to melt in the winter sunshine. Outside, a flock of chickadees gamboled through the naked branches of the locust tree.

The small register in the floor gave up little heat from the downstairs. I was used to the cold. At my house none of the radiators in our bedrooms worked. We also had bare floors with handmade rag rugs on either side of the beds and a potty sitting on an island of its own. My brass bed was the same as Kiko's and Yuki's, with a thin mattress and flat springs covered with newspapers for insulation. Our mothers piled blankets on top of us and wondered why we were still cold.

On Yuki's half of the room were rows of teddy bears and dolls with cracked heads. She slept with her dog, Hanako. I wanted a picture of the little dog and little girl sharing the same pillow, but my Kodak box camera was good only for outdoor shots in bright sunshine and I needed to focus my new camera from under a black cloth with the subject surrounded by reflector lamps.

Kiko's mother looked in, chattering in Japanese. She wore her black hair in a bun, as my mother did, but with large combs, and her cotton dresses were covered by huge aprons.

"Up, up," she cried as she tapped Yuki awake and stroked the dog. She shook my arm in a rough but kindly way and poked under the covers for Kiko.

Kiko stretched herself awake. She is like a flower, I thought, smelling of violets and velvety to the touch, her hair shiny as wet coal. The Japanese-American girls at Garfield High had worn their hair in Dutch bobs with bangs, but after we graduated, Kiko let her hair grow two inches below her ears and trained it into a pageboy. What a difference that made.

When Mrs. Nakayama called us from below, we exploded out of bed and into our clothes. It was ten by the kitchen clock, a Kit-Cat with eyes and tail that moved back and forth. We didn't know it then, but at that very moment, just two time zones away in Hawaii, men our age were dying and ships were sinking in a place I had never heard of before—Pearl Harbor.

Mr. Nakayama and his mother were already seated at the long table with the red oilcloth cover. He pulled out a chair for me.

"Robin-chan, you like Japanese chewing gum?" Mr. Nakayama was such a tease. I knew he expected me to wrinkle my nose in distaste, so I picked up a piece of dried squid from the plate and popped it in my mouth. Later, I figured, I could spit it out into my napkin.

After stuffing the range with wood, Kiko's twin brother Tadashi stood at the sink washing his hands.

I stared at his back, remembering how for so long we had been the same height, but in our junior year he had suddenly shot up. When we were freshmen at Garfield he had caught me hanging by my knees from the plum tree in the garden, trying with both hands to keep my dress in place. Oh, how he had grinned at me. Tadashi and his father had that same grin.

When Kiko spotted a spider that had wandered away from the wood box next to the kitchen stove, she chased it with a broom. That poor little creature frantically searched for cover.

I grabbed the broom. "Please, don't kill it."

Tadashi zoomed in like a ballet dancer, caught the spider in a dish towel and gently shook it out the back door.

Kiko shuddered. "I hate spiders. Tad is a better Buddhist than I am."

Mrs. Nakayama served miso soup, cold rice shaped into triangles, little dishes of pickled vegetables, and drumsticks marinated in teriyaki sauce. My rice had long thin strips of green onion on top, bunched up like ribbon on a gift package.

I turned to Kiko. "Your mother is so artistic. She makes me feel like an honored guest in this house, waiting on me and thanking me profusely for everything. I never get that kind of treatment at home. I'm sick and tired of waiting on my father and my brother, Chris. Why can't they get up and get their own knives?"

I hated the old German custom of women waiting on their men. It made me feel like a servant.

Mr. Nakayama nudged me with his elbow. "You like rice?"

"Yes, I do. But my mother doesn't serve rice very often."

"What you eat then?"

"Potatoes. Mashed, fried with onions, baked. I love potato pancakes."

"Akiko like rice all the time. You a potato girl." Mr. Nakayama sneaked another slice of dried squid onto my plate.

Before we were finished with breakfast, Mr. Nakayama's brother arrived. Uncle Shig was offered green tea and rice crackers.

Kiko and I got the giggles while we tidied up the kitchen, so it took twice as long to finish the job. Yuki stood in the doorway, hands on hips, obviously disgusted with us.

"Hurry up. Tadashi and I have the Monopoly game set up."

It was almost noon when the four of us started to play Yuki's favorite game. On the other side of the living room Mrs. Nakayama and Grandmother sat in rocking chairs listening to the two brothers who sounded like bumblebees buzzing against windows. Mr. Nakayama's voice was loud, his gestures flamboyant, his manner authoritative. Uncle Shig was the smaller, shorter, and younger of the two men.

I had just acquired my first hotel when we heard loud thumping on the front door. Tadashi jumped out of his chair.

On the porch stood a uniformed police officer and two men in dark suits who identified themselves as FBI agents. "We're looking for Shigeru Nakayama."

A stunned silence settled over everyone. When Mr. Nakayama began to mumble in Japanese, Uncle Shig cried out, "What have I done to disgrace my family?"

I think it was prophetic that it was Tadashi who took charge of the situation. Not yet nineteen years old, Tadashi was hesitant, almost apologetic in deference to his elders, when he said, "This is my Uncle Shigeru Nakayama. Why are you looking for him?"

"He works for an import company, doesn't he? We're rounding up Japanese nationals. We need to take him downtown for questioning."

The two brothers stood side by side, looking bewildered. Finally, the policeman said, "What's the matter with you people? Haven't you heard the news? Don't you have a radio? Two hours ago the Japs bombed Pearl Harbor, the naval base at Honolulu."

All I could think of was the radio play that had been produced three years ago by Orson Welles about invading Martians. People were scared to death and some got baptized in a hurry. In the aftermath, a congressman warned the nation about the power of radio and its trend toward violence.

"Those Japs have made a hell out of Honolulu," one of the FBI agents exclaimed. "They've sunk ships, destroyed planes, and killed thousands of our men. Mark my words, they'll be bombing Seattle next."

This wasn't a play. This was the real thing. Tadashi looked as though he'd been hit with a baseball bat. Uncle Shig's hands trembled as he picked up his coat and headed for the door.

Kiko and I rushed to the window. Uncle Shig looked back at us, that same startled expression frozen on his face. He followed the men as though he were a dog on a leash.

Kiko began to cry. "I'll never see him again."

"No, Kiko, they'll question him and let him go."

"Are you kidding? If he were your uncle, maybe."

"How did they know where to find him?"

"I'll bet they had him on a list with my father's address."

After the police car disappeared, we turned on the radio and listened with bowed heads to the strident voices: *Our country is united at last... The keep-America-out-of-war organizations are silenced... Senator Burton K. Wheeler of Montana, leader of American anti-war forces, has declared, 'We'll beat the hell out of those Japs.'*

"I've got to go home," I cried. It was as though there had been an earthquake and I needed to know that our house was still standing and my parents were okay. I ran upstairs for my coat and overnight bag. When I came down again, Kiko slipped on a jacket and followed me out the door. The cold air was heavy with wood smoke.

Kiko looked forlorn. "I wish you weren't in such a hurry. Do you blame me for what's happened?"

"Of course not, silly!"

At the bottom of the stairs we sat down, hugging our knees with our skirts touching the ground. I was reluctant to go. Now that Kiko and Tadashi were freshmen at the University of Washington and I was pounding a typewriter for the U.S. Army Engineers downtown, I saw Kiko only on weekends.

"Robin, you probably won't believe this, but last Friday my poly-sci prof told us that he expected Japan to attack us this weekend. He offered to lay bets on it." She fastened her eyes on my face as though she wanted to catch my full reaction.

"Two days ago? How could he have known? That's impossible."

"We laughed at him. We thought he was crazy." Kiko's shoulders slumped. "I'm afraid to go to school tomorrow."

"You've got to go. Your finals are coming up."

"What if people don't distinguish between us and those militarists in Japan? What if they lump us all together?"

"Nobody's going to shoot you."

"What if people get mean and say mean things? People will be hysterical.

The average person in Japan is peace loving just like you and me. It's the militarists that have done this. Look at what they did to China. If they expect to take us over too, they've got another think coming."

I stared at the tips of my shoes that peeked out from under my skirt and said nothing. President Roosevelt had promised the mothers of America that he would keep their boys at home—unless there was an attack. Now he could send them anywhere.

I bent over and whispered in Kiko's ear, "Do you realize what all this means? Our brothers will be drafted. Chris and Tadashi will be going to war."

Sudden realization shocked us into momentary silence.

"Kiko, I think I was a soldier in another life because I've always known how terrible war is. No one had to tell me. I didn't read about it. I've known all my life there's no glory in it." There wasn't anything more to say. I got up, pulled the bandanna from my pocket and tied it under my chin. I started home without looking back and without saying goodbye.

2

It was afternoon when I hurried home from Kiko's house. On this December day roses and geraniums nodded in the front yards of our peaceful neighborhood along Yesler Way.

Perhaps at this very moment, people who had been to church were hearing announcements about the morning's terrible events. Those who didn't have radios, telephones, and automobiles might be out of touch awhile longer.

We were lucky. Our family had a little Philco radio that sat on a table next to my father's chair, a wall phone hanging in the back hall, and an old Dodge car.

When I opened the back door of our house, I was drawn to the living room by Mom's voice. "You've never had any kids. You know nothing about giving them an education."

They were at it again. Uncle Fritz loved to bully Mom until she lost confidence; then she turned sullen and made outrageous remarks. Sometimes, after bursting into tears, she refused to talk to us for hours.

The fact that Uncle Fritz meddled in our family affairs infuriated Mom, but Dad would pat her on the fanny and say, "Have a heart, Daisy. We are all the family he's got."

Today, Dad sat in his chair, sucking his pipe, with his feet propped on the hassock. My brother, Chris, straddled the arm of the davenport, bundled up in an overcoat and stocking cap because he studied for finals in his unheated bedroom.

Mom wore her brown braids in coronet style on Sundays, but already the hairpins were coming loose. "Every quarter it's $30 for registration and $10 for books, not to mention lunches and bus fare," she was telling Uncle Fritz. "All that comes out of Henry's wages, but it really takes two of us to make it, because I get shorthanded on household expenses. So, I go to the Pike Place Market late on Saturdays to get cheap vegetables. I scout out vacant lots for dandelion greens and blackberries. I serve hamburger seven nights a week. I sweat over the canning kettle putting up stuff from my father's garden. Scrimper and scrounger, that's me, but it's the way I help finance Chris' college education. All I ask is to see him graduate."

"Sorry, Daisy, but you're not going to see him graduate. Not by a long shot."

"And why not? He has only two quarters to go."

"He'll never make it to June. I'll bet he gets a notice from the draft board before the end of January."

"We'll sweat it out then."

"No, you won't. Do you want him in the Infantry? That's where he'll go if he doesn't enlist. With his ROTC training, he'll be an officer. He should enlist tomorrow."

I hated Uncle Fritz about now. I wanted him to shut up.

Mom was fighting tears. "I hate war. What did we accomplish with the last one; twenty million dead from Spanish flu alone? Why did we have to get involved in this one? Look at him. Twenty-two years old and perfect. They always take the beautiful and most healthy young men first. I didn't raise you to be cannon fodder, Christopher."

"Good Lord, woman, use your head. We've been attacked. By tomorrow, we'll be involved on two fronts. You'll sing a different tune when the Japs bomb your house."

Chris, who had been nervously tapping his slide rule on his knee, removed his cap and smoothed his hair with his fingers, leaving it tousled.

"Mom, I'm finishing autumn quarter, but I won't be registering for winter quarter. I'm sorry I can't finish the year for you, but I promise I'll wait until after Christmas to enlist. Uncle Fritz is right. By enlisting I can have a choice, and I'm for joining the Air Corps. I want to be a pilot."

Mom sat down hard on the piano stool, and when she rotated it to hide her face, it made a screeching sound.

Dad jumped up to shake Chris' hand. Uncle Fritz draped an arm around my brother's neck.

"You men are all alike," Mom cried, and as she turned the piano stool back, it screeched again. "You love war. Don't try to deny it. When you're young, you can't wait to get into the fight. When you're too old to go, you expect your sons and nephews to do your fighting for you."

Uncle Fritz heaved a loud, exasperated sigh. "What the hell are you talking about? I'm not looking forward to another war. And I wasn't sitting on my backside during the last one either."

I had heard how eagerly these two brothers, in spite of their German ancestry, had looked forward to joining up for World War I. Dad had been devastated when he was rejected because of his eyes. Uncle Fritz made it into the Navy and almost died of influenza after the Armistice was signed.

Chris edged away from Dad and Uncle Fritz. "Mom, I think you and Dad should see Robin through college now that I'm going to be gone."

Uncle Fritz snorted. "For crying out loud, she doesn't need college. She'll get married." Uncle Fritz believed that a woman's place is in the home.

"I'm serious," Chris persisted. "Mr. McDaniels at Garfield said that I'd be better off in a vocational school. He said Robin is college material. I think he'd have gotten her a scholarship if you'd been interested in sending her."

When Chris was excited, his eyes were luminescent and his skin glowed. The girls at Garfield High had thought he was a knockout.

But our parents weren't listening. Dad took off for the basement to stoke the furnace and Mom hurried out to answer the telephone.

"Don't go off half-cocked," Uncle Fritz called after Mom as a parting shot.

When Chris melted out the door, I was left alone with Uncle Fritz.

"How is your friend?" he asked.

I felt the hairs on the back of my neck bristle. "Okay."

"It's too bad her family didn't go back to Japan before this trouble started."

"Why should they? Kiko and her brother and sister were born here. They're citizens."

"You're talking through your hat. I don't care where they were born. The Japs have their ties to Japan. Most of them came here to make a fast buck and go home again. They want Japan to win this war."

"I know lots of Japanese people, Uncle Fritz, and they are just like us. They want to live in peace and make a decent living for their families."

"Then why did they attack Pearl Harbor? You will learn the hard way, my girl. The enemy is in our midst, and I hope they don't destroy us. During the Thirties, I warned people that the Japs were everywhere taking pictures, and no one would listen."

I hoped he wasn't going to get on the subject of the yellow peril and the decline of the white race.

If there was anything I wanted passionately in life it was to become a knowledgeable and articulate person. I wanted to beat Uncle Fritz in an argument. I didn't want to hurt him. He'd been good to Chris and me when we were kids, taking us to the circus and sideshows and buying us cotton candy and Karmel-Korn. But I remembered also the shock of seeing a deer strapped to the hood of his car.

When Dad returned to the living room, I studied him and Uncle Fritz. Dad wore horn-rimmed glasses with thick lenses that magnified his eyes. Uncle Fritz was better looking, for sure.

They were beginning to show their age, and because of that they reminded me of Grandpa Mueller who had come from Germany as a young man. Grandpa had had little education, but he yearned for knowledge. After trying to read Hegel and Kant, he confessed to me that he got headaches "reading dem guys."

Dad told the story of Grandpa getting into a fight with a neighbor. A judge put them both in a "nut house." Grandpa loved it. "A great experience," he said, "and it didn't cost me nussing." When he grew a potbelly, he showed everybody. "See how my gut is getting out?" And he complained about his co-workers at the shipyard, "Dose udder guys do half-assed jobs and bullshoot all the time." I missed Grandpa.

After Uncle Fritz left, Dad spent the rest of the afternoon trying to black out the windows. An impossible job, I thought, as I scanned the high ceilings and big windows of our Victorian house. The ugly green blinds did the trick all right except for the light that leaked along the edges. Mom had heard a newsman on the radio warn that a lighted cigarette could be seen a mile away.

With my blouses and skirts pressed for the week and six pair of silk stockings dripping on the back porch, I was free to spend the rest of the day as I liked, but as long as the radio blared, I couldn't practice the piano. I wrapped myself in an old bathrobe and cuddled down in my big chair to read, but couldn't concentrate on my book.

After supper, I arranged trays of developer and fixing solution on a card table in the bathroom, screwed in an amber light bulb, and plugged in my printing box. I liked seeing the images gradually appear as I gently shook the printing paper in the developer. After a brief rinse, the prints were immersed in the hypo or fixer, and later transferred to the bathtub. After an hour's wash, I laid them out on newspapers to dry. Tomorrow, I would press them with an iron and leave them to flatten in the big dictionary. By then my fingers would be stained brown by the photo chemicals and I would have to bleach them with Clorox.

The first pictures were of our house, to be pasted on Mom's Christmas cards. The photo showed the holly tree, which was as tall as the steeple, and the concrete bulkhead, the cement for which had come around the Horn, Dad said, before the Panama Canal was built.

To keep warm I wore a yellow cardigan with a matching sweater underneath. There were no radiators in the bathroom, probably because former occupants used an outhouse until 1901 when the bathroom was tacked on. The tall tank in the kitchen never got more than lukewarm from the coils in the wood stove. Taking a bath meant heating water in canning kettles, and once in the claw-footed tub of the unheated bathroom, it didn't stay hot very long.

After I laid out the prints on newspapers in the dining room, I hurried into the living room to warm up beside the potbellied stove. The furnace in the basement only took the chill off the house. It was the wood range in the kitchen and the little potbellied stove in the living room that gave us comfort. Mom and I liked to lift our skirts above our knees to expose our legs to that lovely warmth.

Dad had just dropped a large piece of wood into the stove. It made a loud thump, and the sparks erupted like a fireworks display in miniature, followed by puffs of smoke.

Mom sat on the davenport embroidering a pillowslip, using a dozen needles, all with different colored threads, stuck in a pillow beside her. "You should be listening to the radio, Robin. They've been nabbing Japanese up and down the coast. There are enemy subs in the Pacific and people are scared."

As I filled my hot water bottle from the teakettle on the stove, Dad tapped me on the shoulder. "I'd be careful if I were you. You could get into trouble being so thick with the Japanese."

I stared at him, trying to read the eyes behind the thick lenses.

Mom dropped her embroidery in her lap. "It's time for you to terminate your friendship with Kiko. It's for your own good and in the best interest of all of us."

My heart thudded in my head. "I can't do that," I cried. "Kiko is my best friend. I would hate myself if I made her unhappy."

I knew they were dead wrong. I think they knew it too, because they didn't say anything more. I pressed the air out of the hot water bottle and tightened the top. Then I said goodnight and went to bed.

3

I'll never forget the morning after the war began. I woke up to utter quiet, the blackout still in force; all radios were silent, not even a dog barked.

Outside my window was a dead city shrouded in black. The first sounds were of Dad cleaning out the clinkers in the furnace. When I smelled coffee, I knew that Mom was up.

By the time I finished breakfast the buses were coming regularly up the hill. There was a stir of excitement aboard, partly because we had an excuse for being late to work.

As I jumped off on Third Avenue and Marion, I turned up my coat collar. The buildings were drenched with fog and swinging on the wind high above them were sea gulls, raucously calling, while little gusts dipped low enough to chase leaves in circles on the sidewalk.

I threaded my way through the lobby of the Central Building past the crowded elevators to the stairs. Eight of us worked for the Dictaphone pool of the U.S. Army Engineers in the southwest corner of the open basement. Already a crew was blacking out the windows.

Goldie Mae, our supervisor, sat at her desk manicuring her nails. Goldie Mae referred to herself as "that peroxide blonde from San Antonio, Texas," happily married but childless. She and her husband had frequented speakeasies in Prohibition days. I suspected that they liked to drink, even though Goldie Mae referred to liquor as "devil's urine."

"My husband is depressed about the war. His chin falls so low, he stumbles over it." She picked up a cylinder from the wire basket and handed it to me. "This is left over from Saturday, honey, so it won't be very exciting. Sure wish I could be a fly on the wall and listen to what's going on upstairs."

I pushed the cylinder into the machine that stood to the left of my typewriter, tapped the foot pedal to turn it on, and adjusted the earphones. At the same time, I counted out onionskin and eleven new carbons and fed the thick packet into my typewriter.

I loved to type. I'm sure that practicing scales and Hanon exercises on the piano since the age of five helped me become a good typist. I managed a hundred words a minute with very few errors. Goldie Mae liked to give me the conversations between Colonel Goertz, our Head Engineer, and Colonel Talley in Alaska because my copies weren't smudgy.

Gina's desk was next to mine and we faced each other over our typewriters. I had known Gina only a couple of months, but already we were fast friends and the youngest members of the pool.

"When I heard about the war, I felt as though the bottom had dropped out of my life. It's a long commute from Mukilteo to Seattle; so I came into town last night, afraid there'd be no bus service this morning. I spend weeknights with my aunt on Capitol Hill." Gina's eyebrows arched beautifully over brown eyes. She didn't pluck hers to a fine line like so many girls did.

When there was a lull in the work, we talked or read the books we kept in our top drawers. Gina was reading *Gone With The Wind*. I told her about my experiences yesterday with the Nakayama family.

"How did you meet Kiko?" Gina wanted to know.

"When we were freshmen in Gym class. Kiko and I hated it. We were self-conscious and the teacher picked on us all the time. Kiko and I got together because we were miserable. That summer her mother dressed me up in one of her kimonos and I was the only Hakujin to dance in their Bon Odori festival."

It had been exciting to dance to the rhythm of the big drum, surrounded by colorful costumes and flashing fans. I jumped up to demonstrate the stylized movements of the coal miner's dance.

"Are these religious dances?" asked Clara who sat opposite us and had been listening to our conversation.

"They're Japanese folk dances, performed at Buddhist festivals. Kiko and her family are Buddhists."

"Does your religion allow you to dance in their festival?"

"Well, of course. Why not?" I distrusted this older woman who looked down her nose at everybody, especially Gina and me.

Gina winked at me. "What a wonderful experience you've had. Not many of us are lucky enough to get to know people of other cultures unless we're in the diplomatic corps."

"Kiko's parents are Issei, born in Japan and considered aliens in this country. Kiko and her brother, Tadashi, and little sister, Yuki, are Nisei or second generation Japanese born here and they are citizens. Kiko and Tadashi are in their first quarter at the University of Washington. Kiko got a scholarship of $50 per quarter from a women's club and that covers her registration and books with a little money to spare. I sure miss her."

"Robin, you're going to have to save your money so you can go to college too."

Gina and I pulled out our Thermos bottles and tore the wax paper loose from our sandwiches. While we ate lunch, Goldie Mae came to each of us with the news that President Roosevelt had declared war on Japan. She hovered over Clara, and in a loud whisper said, "You know that engineer with the cookie duster? Well he got one of the girls in Payroll pregnant. He's lower than a snake slithering in the gutter." Then she flounced off, leaving a trail of Shalimar perfume.

By late afternoon the cylinders were rolling in, most of them recordings of conversations with engineers in Alaska. They were prefaced with a warning from the censor: THE ENEMY IS LISTENING – GUARD YOUR WORDS ACCORDINGLY.

"I'm worried about Kiko," I told Gina during another lull. "I'm going to stop at her house on the way home because I need to know how she got along today. She doesn't have a phone. Mr. Nakayama is very stubborn about not wanting a phone or a car."

"Where is Yesler Way?"

I waved in the direction of south. "You must have seen that steep hill on the other side of the County-City Building. During pioneer days, that was the original skid road for logs on their way to Yesler's mill. Before that, it was an Indian trail used to transport canoes between Puget Sound and Lake Washington."

I paused. Gina seemed to be listening intently.

"In the Twenties, immigrants settled in the neighborhoods around Yesler Way, mostly Jews from the Isle of Rhodes and Russians who had fled the Revolution. I played with little girls who couldn't speak English, but in a day or two they were fluent enough to fool anybody. Our neighbor from Hungary left her little boy in a childcare center on her first day in the United States while she looked for a job. When she picked him up, he came running, shouting, 'Where have you been, you son of a gun?'"

Gina laughed. She was such a good listener that I was inspired to go on and on.

"The old mansions at the top of the hill have recently been replaced with a housing project. Before they were demolished, artists from all over town came to paint those old houses. Now on our bus route we have kosher markets, Finnish baths, a Chinese laundry, a Japanese grocery store, Father Divine's Son Bill's Place, and the Bikur Cholim Synagogue."

"Fantastic," was Gina's comment.

I plunged on. "Yesler was a cable line until a couple of years ago. My Dad called it the 'garlic special.' A gripman and a brakeman stood on each end of the cable car, managing the huge levers that gripped the cable stretching from Third Avenue to Lake Washington and back. You could see the cable through the narrow opening in the street. It hummed like a waterfall. When the line shut down at one a.m., the silence made my ears ring."

We were interrupted by Goldie Mae's booming voice. "I hate politicians," she was telling one of the girls. "They're so tied up in their own umbilical cords that they're strangling and purple in the face."

❀

I caught the early bus. When I knocked at Kiko's house Yuki's little dog, Hanako, threw herself at the door in a frenzy of barking. Yuki opened the door, scooped up the dog and carried her away.

Mr. Nakayama beckoned me in. "Big blackout tonight. No radio," he told me as he adjusted a paper shield on the window.

Grandmother sat with folded hands. "Konban-wa, Obachan," I said, and the old lady nodded.

Kiko and Tadashi studied in a room adjacent to the living room, which had been a sun porch. A lamp sat on the table between them, its top shaped like a pyramid, with beads hanging from its metal frame. There was a blind typewriter at one end of the table, like the one I used to play with when I was a kid.

"So you had to come check on us." Kiko's eyes were floating black discs. She looked smart in her school clothes, a gray skirt and red sweater. "Well, nothing momentous happened to us today, but if looks were bullets, I'd be dead."

Tadashi teetered on the back legs of his chair, the cuffs of his white shirt rolled up to his elbows. "Yosh spent last night in jail. He went to Portland with a bunch from the church to perform for the Buddhists there, but the news about Pearl Harbor got them worried, so halfway through the show, they quit and headed home."

Kiko interrupted him. "Even though they were all Nisei, the police stopped their bus in Chehalis for moving aliens across a state line, and they went to jail."

"I don't get it," I broke in. "Why did they go to jail?"

I could tell when Tadashi felt impatient with his twin. "Someone gave the okay this morning for them to come home, so why the big fuss?"

I stared at them. They were beautiful, with smooth, golden skin, but their dispositions were so different. Kiko was a complainer, dissident, reformer, and alarmist. She made me mad about injustices in the world. But Tadashi accepted adversity without a quarrel. He made me feel good about life.

When Kiko rushed off to help her mother, Tadashi offered to see me to the bus. As he opened the door, I remembered coming to this house four years ago as a tomboy climbing trees. Now I was a young workingwoman in high heels, carrying an umbrella and a purse large enough to accommodate a Thermos bottle, lunch, and book, along with money, lipstick, and comb. I glanced at my new patent leather pumps. Goldie Mae said they showed off pretty ankles. Because of the weather, Mom would probably scold me for not having worn my galoshes.

Tadashi looked sidewise at me as we stepped out into a misty rain that felt like a gentle kiss on my cheek. "Akiko got an A on her term paper. She says your typing made a difference in her grade."

"She could have taken typing when I did, but she wanted Zoology. Why is it that every college prep student I've known hasn't wanted to learn to type?"

"Robin, college students don't want to end up as clerks. Akiko says you're saving your money for college. What's your major going to be?"

"I don't know. There aren't many openings for women: nurse, librarian, teacher, social worker—that's about it, and I don't want to be any of those."

"You should go just for the heck of it. Forget about jobs. That's what college is about."

"Kiko will probably be in graduate school by the time I get there. I miss seeing her every day."

Tadashi laughed. "Mr. Harrison used to call you two the Siamese twins."

"Oh, him." I wrinkled my nose in disgust. "He told my father that I was smart enough, considering my age and sex. I think he hated girls. I had to work twice as hard for a decent grade."

"At least he said you're smart. When we were freshmen, he dragged Yosh and me out of study hall by the ears and took us to the Principal's office."

We sloshed through wet leaves, while big drops from the trees splattered loudly on my umbrella. It was dark without the streetlights to guide us. Some of the passing cars had new yellow covers on their headlights.

Tadashi grabbed the umbrella when my arm began to sag. "You've been good for Akiko. She used to be painfully shy until you came along."

When we reached the bus stop he turned and faced me. "This afternoon I went down to the recruiting office to enlist and they turned me down."

I gasped. "What do you mean?"

"I wanted to join the Army, but they rejected me."

"But, why?"

"I'm classified as C-4, an enemy alien. It's as though I'm not really an American. That means I have no country. I never wanted to go to Japan. I don't give three hoots about Japan."

The light from a passing automobile revealed his face for an instant. He looked both embarrassed and angry. "I've been exploding with this news and had no one to tell it to. I don't want my family to learn that I was rejected."

I didn't know what to say. I guess that's why I reached up to hug him. He dropped the umbrella and put his arms around me. For some reason, I began to cry. And there we were, he trying to comfort me when I had meant to comfort him.

When the bus rasped up the hill, Tadashi picked up the umbrella, took my arm, and guided me to the curb. I stumbled onto the bus, feeling a rush of excitement as the token jingled in the fare box. I looked back. Tadashi stood motionless, a dark shadow on the sidewalk.

4

I didn't see Tadashi again until his and Kiko's birthday. In the meantime, I tried to read a biography of suffragette Lucretia Mott, attend a photography class, and practice finger exercises on the piano.

I suppose I was being childish about the war, acting as though it had been trumped up just for my inconvenience. I didn't want to read or talk about it, especially after one of our Garfield boys turned up missing in action.

On December 9th, two days after the war started, mobs gathered downtown to extinguish lights left on in window displays. One woman kicked out a window in a show of patriotism. For five nights the blackouts were rigidly enforced.

When Germany and Italy declared war on the United States, Uncle Fritz fumed. "England had to get us in to fight her battles, as if she didn't get fat enough starving India."

By the end of the first week, Dad glowered and pounded the table. "Isn't there anything we can talk about except war?"

I usually spent Saturday afternoons with Kiko. We picnicked at the park, ate five-cent hot dogs at Rhodes' dime store, or went to a movie or the Art Museum. On December 13th, we explored the labyrinth of the Pike Place Market and I bought clams to take to Mrs. Nakayama. She appreciated them more than candy.

I found Mr. Nakayama glowering just like Dad. "What's the matter with your father?" I asked Kiko as we set the table.

"He's furious because Tad bought a Model A Ford from someone who enlisted. It cost him $50, a month's wages in the cannery, enough to take care of one quarter's tuition, books, and bus fare. My father says that soon it'll be impossible to get gasoline, so the car will be a white elephant."

I knew why Tadashi had bought the car. For fear of revealing too much, I changed the subject. "I read in the paper that the banks have frozen Japanese assets."

"My father still collects rents at the hotel, but who knows how long that will last."

"Kiko, I've saved up over $200 since I went to work. That would take care of food for a couple of months. Are we good enough friends that you'd let me know if your family needs help?"

"Yes, Robin, I'll let you know."

"Promise?"

"Yes, I promise."

"And I don't want you to feel obligated to pay it back."

The Japanese had crazy ideas about gift giving. Once I had attended a funeral with Kiko. Everyone gave an envelope containing money for the bereaved family and was given white handkerchiefs in return. Kiko said that meticulous records were kept so that donors would eventually be repaid in kind, and she added, "It's not that gifts are given with strings attached, it's just that they are always received that way."

On December 15th, we learned that the *Arizona* and five other ships had been lost at Pearl Harbor and nearly 3,000 men had died. On December 16th, the first Pearl Harbor photos appeared in the paper. On the 20th, the newspapers reported that submarines had attacked two U.S. ships off the coast of California.

On the 22nd, I hurried from work to the Nakayama home to celebrate the twins' nineteenth birthday. On their four previous birthdays, Mr. Nakayama had taken us out to dinner, and last year he treated us to a special performance of actors from Japan at the Nippon Kan Theater. Sometimes we walked to the restaurant, or a friend took us, and once during bad weather Mr. Nakayama actually hired a taxi.

"We are dining at home tonight," Kiko informed me. "The Chinese are wearing *I am Chinese* buttons and we don't want to run into any of them."

Kiko was closing the butsudan for the night. The shrine was lacquered and trimmed in gold. A small vase of flowers stood on its inner shelf. Each morning, a tiny mound of freshly cooked rice was placed in a small brass container below the statue of Buddha. When Kiko removed the rice and popped it in her mouth, I gasped in astonishment.

Kiko grinned. "It would be a shame to waste it. I've seen my grandmother rescue a single grain of rice because it deserves to fulfill its destiny, she says."

I knew that members of my family would be uncomfortable in a house that contained a Buddha enshrined in a butsudan and a statue of Kwanon in the garden. To them, these were idols of worship; therefore, an evil presence. They would never understand that the statues of Buddha and Kwanon were not idols but representations of compassion, gratitude, and wisdom. I had learned a lot during the four years Kiko and I were best friends.

I was disappointed that we weren't going to Chinatown, or Japantown, as the Japanese knew it. Many buildings had fancy balconies, some sidewalks were wood plank, and the signs in windows of old hotels advertised beds for twenty-five cents a night.

My family never went out to dinner. They were still in the throes of the Depression, as were millions of other people. Probably that is why there were so few restaurants in Seattle, and no Chinese restaurants outside of Chinatown. Uncle Fritz wouldn't have been caught dead in Chinatown.

I always lorded it over my parents with full descriptions of my adventures. "Mr. Nakayama took us to the Golden Pheasant, which is a half block up the hill from Jackson Street on Sixth Avenue. He told me that this building was one of Seattle's first schools. Now it has a canopy that goes all the way from the porch down to the sidewalk. They have curtains across the booths for privacy. For fifty cents apiece, they bring huge platters of food. It's the best food I've ever tasted, and I'm getting pretty good at eating with chopsticks. Besides, it's fun to be waited on." It was hard for me to understand why my parents looked glum on these occasions.

When Tadashi arrived with his friend Yoshio, my heart began to beat real fast. A restaurant dinner would have been wasted on me. I can't remember what we ate. After dinner, I pulled out my camera. "I want a picture," I told them. What I really wanted was a photo of Tadashi to paste on my mirror. I plugged in my photo light, attached it to the back of a chair, adjusted the tabletop tripod, and slipped my head under a black cloth. At first, Tadashi, Kiko and Yoshio were a blur, but gradually I tightened the focus until the upside-down image was clear on the ground-glass screen.

"I need to stand on my head to see you." I felt self-conscious as I ducked out from under the cloth, removed the back of the camera, and replaced it with the film holder.

"Why don't we get our father to take the picture so you can be in it," Tadashi suggested.

"Where did you get this camera?" Yoshio wanted to know.

"My Uncle Fritz gave it to me."

"He must have bought it in a pawn shop. It's old fashioned. There are much better cameras on the market now and you should buy one before the supply runs out."

Tadashi broke in, "You'll never find a better lens, Robin. Your pictures are so clear and detailed. Don't ever throw that camera away."

"Where's yours?"

"It was confiscated a few days ago."

I felt my face flush with anger. "The government took your new camera?"

Tadashi nodded. "They took our radios, too. Luckily, we didn't have any guns."

25

Tadashi left the table and returned with a rolled-up piece of butcher paper. "Maybe it's a good thing that I lost my camera. I'm drawing again." When he unrolled the paper, I saw dozens of little human figures in black with swashes of brown in the background. I loved it.

"You're an artist!" I cried.

He grinned and waved his hand. "Not yet."

When Mr. Nakayama put on his coat and hat, Tadashi explained. "He's going to the loyalty rally at the church. Why don't we go too?"

Kiko and I trailed Tadashi and Yoshio out the door.

"I bet you're glad finals are over. Have they sent out your grades yet?"

Kiko shook her head.

"What are you taking next quarter?"

"Tad and I aren't going back to school winter quarter. We'll learn how to do our father's work at the hotel in case the FBI takes him. Every day someone we know disappears. Even some of our Buddhist ministers are gone. The FBI never thinks about the women and children left behind. Our father says that he has seen Japanese women eating out of garbage cans. Anyway, my scholarship has been cancelled."

"How awful."

"Forget it. Maybe I'll make enough money to go back for spring quarter."

As we neared the temple, we could see that the building was packed, the steps leading to the hondo crowded with young Japanese males.

A friend of Yoshio's appeared. "Everybody's swearing their loyalty to the government. Of course we are loyal. Why should we have to prove it?"

In October, only two months ago, I had witnessed the dedication ceremony for this new building at 14th and Main. There had been a procession with shrine-bearers dressed in white carrying the golden butsudan. Yuki had marched with the Girl Scouts. Anxious adults had herded along little girls and boys in colorful court costumes. Now, what would happen to this beautiful building?

At Tadashi's insistence, we headed for the drugstore on Jackson Street for chocolate sodas.

"You might as well enjoy these while they last," Mr. Weed, the druggist, said as he prepared our drinks and we dangled our legs from the tall metal chairs. "Sooner or later, there'll be shortages and the first one will be sugar."

I studied the far reaches of the store in the huge mirror behind the fountain. Mr. Weed wasn't the best housekeeper. A ragged pile of *Life* magazines waited on the counter to be distributed to their proper place. Underfoot was a wood floor, heavily oiled, with dust balls accumulating in corners. I was disappointed when the last of my drink gurgled in the bottom of my glass.

As we prepared to leave, Tadashi leaned forward to tell me a joke and I fell in step with him. At that moment, a man in a red plaid coat blocked our way out.

"Lousy Japs. I'd like to see all of you lined up against a wall." He raised his arms and pretended to take aim at each of us in turn. When his attention centered on me, he scowled. "What in Sam Hill do you think you're doing? You ought to be strung up by the ears and left to hang. Jap-loving bitch!"

I looked into this man's ugly red face, my back prickled and I thought my knees would buckle. I expected him to strike me and then I knew things would fly and Mr. Weed's store would be a shambles.

"Shall we take him?" Yoshio whispered.

"No," was Tadashi's answer.

Mr. Weed's voice sounded far off. "These are loyal American citizens. Leave them alone."

"They're yellow scum." The man moved closer and raised his fists.

The standoff ended when four people pushed into the drugstore. Tadashi and Yoshio grabbed me and propelled me through the open door. We walked quickly and silently back to the Nakayama home where the

Model A was parked. Tadashi opened the door to the rear seat and helped me in. Kiko followed.

By this time I was fighting tears. Was I an embarrassment to them? When we got to my house, I was angry. "Aren't you going to say anything about what happened back there?"

Yoshio opened the door for me. "Robin, some other time."

"Don't try to shut me up. In my whole life, I've never been so scared."

"You needn't have been," Tadashi assured me. "Yosh and I are skilled in martial arts. We can kick like kangaroos."

"We could've shown him a thing or two."

"Of course we were in danger." Kiko's eyes blazed. "If we'd tried to defend ourselves, we'd have been in big trouble. Can't you see the headline? Young Japs Gang Up On White Man In Drug Store. Robin, not too many years ago, a Hakujin could kill a Japanese and get away with it."

We were quiet for a moment and then I said, "I've never been treated with hostility before."

As I stepped out of the car, Yoshio jostled my arm. "Consider yourself initiated, Robin. Now you know how it feels to have a waiter spit in your soup."

5

At breakfast, as I joined my parents for toast and soft-boiled eggs, I heard Dad say, "It's going to be a bleak Christmas." Mom plunked down the *Post-Intelligencer* with a thump, one finger marking her place in Eleanor Roosevelt's *My Day* column.

"Not on your life. We still have sugar in the larder. No one we know is being pulled out of the mud at Pearl Harbor. And we aren't having to entertain Winston Churchill and eighty other guests like poor Mrs. Roosevelt."

As I finished my breakfast, Mom continued the morning digest. "Violet says someone she knows has a barrage balloon waving around above her house like a big fat slug. The Army installed it in the vacant lot next to their house one night while they were asleep. Now, several soldiers are encamped there guarding the balloon."

I slipped out the front door with my overnight bag, wishing I could get an earlier start on the Christmas Eve festivities at Grandpa and Grandma's house at Indianola. Dad would be dismissed early in the afternoon from his job in the City Treasurer's office at the County-City Building, but those of us who worked for the War Department could expect to work a full day.

So, it was dark when I darted out of the Central Building where I worked and ran down the steep hill on Marion Street to First Avenue and over the footbridge to Colman Dock. The ferry to Indianola left at 5:20 p.m. I made it aboard the *Illahee* seconds before the man on the slip wound the winch that raised the apron above the car deck. The skipper sounded a loud *boop* as the ferry slowly churned into Elliott Bay.

I climbed to the upper deck, leaned on the rail, and watched the waterfront recede as the ferry got underway. The city, which Aunt Vi described as "best lighted in the nation," was gloomy and dark. The Smith Tower, "tallest building west of the Mississippi," was barely visible against the night sky. Only a few lights flickered on the oily black water of the harbor.

I tried to imagine how Seattle looked before the tide flats were filled in to make room for railroad tracks and docks. Once, Aunt Vi took my cousin, Frannie, and me to the spot where the Denny cabin once stood to see the roses blooming at the edge of a parking lot, progeny of those planted by Louisa Boren Denny in the 1850s. According to Aunt Vi, at the time of the Battle of Seattle in 1853, when Chief Leschi led Indian warriors against the pioneers, Louisa fled the cabin with her baby on one arm and a batch of biscuits on the other, and sought refuge on a ship anchored in the harbor.

A young man stood at the rail beside me. He had a nice straight nose and a haystack of blond hair. "Hi," he said. "Do you remember the *Hyak*? It used to make a two-hour run from Seattle to Poulsbo, stopping at Indianola, Suquamish, and Lemolo on the way. In the mid-thirties the ferries replaced the steamers. I hated to see the steamers go. I didn't want that era to end."

Yes, I remembered the *Hyak*. It was cold and windy on deck, so I turned to go inside and he followed me. I found myself a seat and he sat down opposite me and leaned forward with his elbows balanced on his knees.

"My grandfather was a captain on a schooner, part of the codfish fleet that sailed to Alaska each summer. Winters, the ships were moored on the east side of Lake Union. When I was sixteen I was in the fish-dressing gang on the *Sophia Christenson* the summer of 1936. It was great. Unfortunately, the schooners were doomed. My father had already become a skipper on a tugboat, and my grandfather was retiring, and the crew didn't much care one way or the other. But I hated to see the sailing ships disappear from Puget Sound."

"That's the way I felt about the street cars, especially the old cable cars."

"I think we have a lot in common. Do you by any chance write poetry?"

I shook my head. He pulled out a packet of crumpled papers and handed them to me. I flattened them out on the bench and read some of them. They were really good. "I like this one about peace."

"That's my credo. I'm a conscientious objector." He made the statement with pride, although with some wariness.

"Really?" I was interested in him now.

"I put in an appeal on my draft classification and if it is granted, I'll enter a Civilian Public Service camp soon. CPS projects are in forestry or soil erosion control. I'm a junior at the U, majoring in Anthropology. I registered for winter quarter on the chance that my number won't come up for awhile."

"How do your parents feel about your being a CO?"

He made a face. "My father and all my relatives on the Olympic Peninsula call me a 'yellow belly.' I'm one lonely pacifist among a lot of super patriots." He gathered up his papers and jammed them into his pocket. "I joined the Society of Friends when I was a freshman. The Friends started the Pacifist movement and they believe that people will eventually learn to live in cooperative brotherhood."

"Don't you think some wars are necessary?" I could hear Uncle Fritz asking that question.

"Not any more. Have you read *Merchants of Death*? That book gives you the scenario of war—the fight for money and power—and the little guys get conned into killing each other."

"What about Hitler and Mussolini?"

He sighed deeply. "If people refused to kill their brethren, the dictators wouldn't have anybody to do their dirty work for them. We've got to start somewhere." He had a nervous habit of punching his left palm with his right fist. "People call this a good war. There are no good wars."

"You are probably right," I said reservedly. "Ideally, neither Christians nor Buddhists believe in killing. Yet, most everyone accepts war as the inevitable way to solve problems. People are bundles of contradictions."

"I think you're on your way to becoming a pacifist!" he declared. "Would you like for me to send you some books and articles? Soon we'll be spending half our national income on this war. The new tax law calls for the highest rates in U.S. history. Did you see the warning in the paper to people earning $15 a week or more? In 1940, only three million Americans made enough to pay income tax."

As I listened to him on the hour-long trip to Indianola, I was impressed. "You should be a teacher," I told him.

"I'm going to be a professor."

When the ferry signaled the dock at Indianola, he offered to carry my bag to the lower deck. "I'm David Engstrom. I wish you'd write to me. It would be a comfort to hear from someone open-minded like you. As it is, I'm an embarrassment to my family and friends."

I pulled out a card left over from my graduation announcements and under Robin Mueller, penned my address and phone number.

The pilings screeched as the ferry scraped against them. Deckhands scurried to secure the ropes, and after the chain dropped, the half-dozen passengers destined for Indianola surged forward with me trailing. Because of the low tide, it was a steep climb up the ramp to the dock.

Halfway up it occurred to me that I might have invited David to share Christmas with us. I was sure he'd rather come with me than go home to his unsympathetic family. But then, maybe my family would be unsympathetic too. They'd embarrassed me enough in the past.

Chris and my cousin Frannie were waiting for me. Aunt Vi called her daughter Frances; Frannie's friends called her Fran, but to me she would always be Frannie. My earliest memories of her were those of us shaking the bars of our playpen. Later, when we were little kids in bloomers, we chased each other around the block on scooters and tried to force each other off the sidewalk. She was "cute as a bug's ear," as Grandma phrased it, with soft brown hair, long lashes trained back with an eyelash curler and daubed with mascara, and spit curls stiffened with blue gelatin and pasted to her cheeks. She liked to chew gum and snap it.

Chris led us up the long dock with a flashlight. He had driven Grandpa's old jalopy, the one with the rumble seat. After parking it in the woods next to the road, we scrambled out and down the crooked path to the kitchen door, brushing against Grandma's maidenhair ferns which grew a yard high like green lace on tall black stems.

Inside were wood-warmth and the aroma of clams and scones. Three lemon pies with snowy tops sat on the counter. The family was already seated at the big, round oak table that took five leaves at holiday time with Grandma's best linen tablecloth glistening on top.

Everyone looked up as I entered, but Aunt Vi was the only one who spoke to me. "Honeybun, I'm glad you finally made it."

First, I toured the living room. Grandma had lined the mantle with hemlock and western yew boughs that had fallen during the big November storm. The Christmas tree was hung with baubles she made by molding a mixture of sugar and egg white inside the two halves of a rubber ball and uniting the halves. Each ball had a peephole for viewing a tiny snow scene inside.

"They're darling!" I exclaimed as I kissed Grandma's dry cheek.

When I sat down, a large bowl of chowder appeared before me. The babble of voices reminded me of a convention of crows in a tall tree. I tuned out the conversation while looking over my spoon at this motley group of relatives who, by accident of birth or marriage, had been thrown together.

Grandpa and Grandma had four daughters—Daisy, Violet, Rose and Pansy. We hadn't seen Rose or Pansy for years. No one talked about them.

33

My mom and Frannie's mother were like two birds prancing back and forth on the same perch, endlessly chirping at one another. Summers, they lay on the beach and got brown as madrona bark and laughed and giggled all day long. When they got mad at their husbands, one or the other would exclaim, "That's just like a man!"

Grandpa had been a logger in his younger days. "I was a member of the Industrial Workers of the World," he boasted on occasion. "That's the infamous I.W.W. The 'I Won't Work' people—a Wobbly, in other words. I struggled to give men a break in their war against the lumber barons." Then he would sing one of the old Joe Hill songs. I couldn't understand why Grandpa believed in men's rights, but was opposed to women working.

"Wake up and die right." Frannie nudged me with an elbow and pushed the wild blackberry jam in my direction.

I stared momentarily at Frannie's father who sat directly across from me. His name was Telford, but Aunt Vi called him Tolly. Uncle Tolly had jowls like a Coho salmon. He was Norwegian, yet he would say, "Never trust a Swede." He demanded an accounting of every nickel Aunt Vi spent. Somehow, Aunt Vi managed to squirrel away a few dollars in a brass teapot just like my mother did in an old cookie jar. This was the only money they could call their own.

"The Northwest will never be the same with all those Okies and Arkies pouring into Seattle to get defense jobs," complained Uncle Fritz, who was depressed by the war news. His jokes about Catholics, Jews and Negroes made me squirm. Years ago he talked endlessly about Versailles. He claimed that Germany had been mistreated after World War I. He was an isolationist then. I could remember when Uncle Fritz actually praised Hitler. *Arbeit! Arbeit!* Everyone had jobs in Germany. But, after Pearl Harbor, he changed his tune.

Dad and Uncle Fritz didn't look like brothers. Uncle Fritz had verve and Dad was dull. Uncle Tolly was dull. How had Mom and Aunt Vi managed to get stuck with such dull, dull men? I had to admit they didn't drink, gamble, or play around, and somehow they had provided their families with the necessities during the Depression without going on the dole. I supposed that the Depression was now officially over. So what was worse—depression or war?

"Daddy, have you any new commuter stories to tell us?" Mom was orchestrating the dinner conversation.

Grandpa gently poked a cigar stub into his pipe and lit it. "Last week, Wade Johnson's cat died. Having read romantic stories about burials at sea the boy thought that would be a fitting tribute to his pet, so he asked his father to do the honors. Mr. Johnson placed the body in a paper sack next to his attaché case intending to dump it over the rail before the ferry docked, but he talked to other commuters and forgot. The bag ended up with his hat on a shelf above the coat rack at work. On his way home, he forgot again. His wife looked in the sack and found two chickens. No one knows who got the cat."

Grandpa stroked his mustache while we laughed. "This week the kids in the village speared dogfish at night and left their bloody carcasses on the dock so the commuters had to hop, skip, and jump their way to the ferry."

We had heard about the women who came aboard in their nightgowns and dressed themselves out of shopping bags. Grandpa made fun of those who overslept their stop at Indianola until it happened to him one night and he had to be rescued out of Suquamish by automobile.

After dinner, we women cleared the dining room and kitchen while the men gravitated to the living room to talk politics. Sometimes they were boring and sometimes they got angry and shouted at each other. Once I tried to join them by reciting facts I had learned in Civics class and they ignored me as though I wasn't there. It was the last time I tried to muscle in.

Uncle Fritz's voice had a carrying quality that was annoying. Now he was complaining about the peace mongers demanding disarmament when this country should have been in full production of war materials. "The National Guard in Everett has no ammunition and their rifles go back to World War I. How can men be trained without modern equipment?" After a while, he griped about Roosevelt. "I hate that man with his CCC and his WPA and his NRA. Blast his hide. And that woman of his—she gets my goat!"

Grandpa tolerated Dad and Uncle Fritz, but I'm sure he didn't like them much, probably because they were German and he was English. Once I heard him call them "krauts." The man he hated most lived in far-away Italy. Grandpa had nothing good to say about the Pope.

With Grandpa and Dad sucking cigars and Uncle Fritz and Uncle Tolly puffing cigarettes, the room turned blue. When Grandma started to cough, the men opened the doors and aired out the house.

Mom and Aunt Vi gave Chris a hug every chance they got and the men actually invited his opinion on subjects of world importance. We were all aware that this was Chris' last Christmas at home.

Chris had retreated behind a *National Geographic* and Frannie was fast asleep on the floor in front of the fireplace when I joined Grandma, Aunt Vi and Mom. They were talking about the funny things children say and do. What I did was unplanned. I don't know what got into me, but I started asking questions about a very touchy subject.

"Grandma, how many cousins do we have in California?"

She looked surprised, but she smiled at me. "You have five cousins, all younger than you."

"Why don't we ever see them? Why don't they come up to Washington to visit us?"

Aunt Vi sashayed around the room in a nervous tizzy, dumping ashtrays and smoothing the tablecloth. Mom hissed at me: "Shame on you." The men stopped talking to listen in.

"Your cousins never come up to see us because their mothers were disinherited."

"Disinherited? Why?"

"Your Aunt Rose got the first divorce in the family. It's old hat nowadays, but a divorce was a disgrace when we were raising our family."

"What happened to her?"

"She remarried, and from what I hear she is happy in her second marriage."

"And Aunt Pansy?"

"Well, Pansy ran off with a gambler. She's still with her gambler, if that's what he really is."

It was so quiet in the room; I could hear my heart beat in my ears. "Those episodes in your life must have hurt a lot. And it must have hurt them too."

"Yes, it did."

"Is there any chance of being reunited with them?"

"I can only hope so."

Mom was furious with me. She muttered, "You're making a reputation for yourself, young lady."

But I wasn't to be stopped. "If I were to marry a Japanese, would the family disinherit me?"

At first Grandma laughed, then she gasped and turned serious. "If I'm still alive, I'll fight for you." She looked around the room as if she were making sure to be heard, especially by Grandpa. "Next July I'm going to California. By then I'll have enough egg money saved up to make the trip by train." She looked happy as she made this announcement.

I had run out of questions. Aunt Vi was quick to fill the void. "I think our working girls want to hit the hay before long, so let's open presents," she suggested as she passed out the divinity and popcorn balls.

After the good wrappings had been salvaged and the rest burned in the fireplace, and all our presents were piled neatly in corners and behind chairs, Mom asked, "Who wants to play pinochle?" Chris excused himself and headed for the guesthouse. Frannie and I climbed to our bunks in the attic.

As we fell asleep, Frannie and I could hear the pinochle players cracking silly jokes and laughing uproariously.

6

It was cold around the edges on Christmas day. Grandpa kept Dad and Uncle Tolly busy bringing alder from the woodshed for the kitchen range and the fireplace. Mom and Aunt Vi helped Grandma with the turkey.

I tried to warm up by the fireplace. There were three stockings hanging from the mantel that we had ignored the night before. Aunt Vi stuffed them every year even though Chris was twenty-two years old and Frannie and I were almost nineteen. I knew from the bulges that by the time we had devoured the candy we would find oranges in the toes of our stockings, symbol of the day not too many years ago, according to Aunt Vi, when that fruit was a rare treat. Grandma remembered when her father came home with an orange and cut it into six pieces so each of his children could have a taste.

During the Depression, Chris, Frannie, and I were luckier than most of our playmates. There'd always been something under the tree for us and we were never hungry thanks to Grandpa's garden and fruit trees, clams from the beach, and wild blackberries from the woods. Once, Dad bought a big salmon for a quarter and Mom said there wasn't enough money in the house to buy a lemon. Things had been that tough sometimes.

When Frannie joined us for breakfast, she looked like a model out of *Vogue* with new slacks bought with money she earned as receptionist in a dental clinic.

"If you're going for a walk, you'd better take off those shoes," Aunt Vi warned her.

With a sigh, Frannie knelt down to search the boot box for last summer's Keds. I was already in Grandma's clodhoppers and an old jacket. Frannie looked me up and down. "Those clam-diggers are so baggy. Why don't you go shopping with me some time? I'd buy you slacks with a crease," and she indicated how neatly her slacks fit.

I felt my cheeks flush with anger just like they did in our younger days when we were called the quarrelsome twosome and Frannie was always hollering, "Robin's got my ball and she won't give it back."

"You've got great possibilities, but you waste them. You've got good hair, but instead of cutting it short, you should wear it long with a pompadour. It's easy to fix. All you do is circle the top of your head with a comb, pull up the hair and fasten the ends with bobby pins. You could train a wave real easy. As it is, you look frumpy."

"Now, Frances, don't you go criticizing Robin." Aunt Vi turned to me with a smile. "You and Chris are brown-eyed with hair the color of honey, a striking combination."

In spite of Aunt Vi, I felt deflated. Frannie loved to change clothes several times a day. Summers, she wore white shorts and showed off her beautiful brown legs. Why didn't I pay more attention to my appearance? I had to remind myself that while Frannie danced in front of the mirror and painted her toenails, I read John Galsworthy's *Forsyte Saga* and Edward Bellamy's *Looking Backward*, books Grandpa had put aside for me. He was the only one in the family who encouraged me to read.

We stepped out into the crisp air. Frannie skipped ahead and down the trail, along a flume that accommodated a stream in winter and was dry in summer. Before the gully opened out to the beach, she stopped and waited for me to catch up.

"Do you remember when our moms wore beach pajamas with big flowers on them? They looked like long dresses, but as time passed, the legs got narrower and narrower until women were actually wearing pants.

Pretty sneaky, don't you think?" She giggled.

Yes, I remembered beach pajamas. Before them, women always wore dresses or skirts. Thanks to the evolution from beach pajamas to pants in the late Twenties and early Thirties, Frannie and I could wear clam diggers or pedal pushers when we were on vacation and even overalls to protect our legs from the wild blackberry vines. Grandma, Mom and Aunt Vi didn't make that transition. They still wore sloppy dresses, some bought for fifty cents during the Depression, and Grandma's long underwear showed when she stooped to weed the garden.

On the beach, we looked across the bay to the northern end of Bainbridge Island. To the west were the Olympic Mountains and to the east, The Mountain, as we always referred to Rainier. The Sound excited memories of excursions into beautiful little bays in Grandpa's rowboat, clam digs, beach fires, and midnight swims. I loved the Sound, wind-swept and turbulent in a squall or smooth and glossy on a summer day. I even loved the muck that squished between my toes as I walked barefoot along the flats at low tide while foul odors exuded from countless organisms in all stages of growth and decay. It was thrilling to hear a blustering storm burgeon across the bay and into the woods and to see the splash and crash of pounding surf while clouds scudded across a dark sky and gulls coasted happily on winter's blast. It was enough to make me cry.

Frannie and I were daughters of the Sound. As toddlers, we had played happily all day with little crabs we found under rocks. Frannie could spot an agate at ten feet, and her pocket would fill with shells and tiny pieces of driftwood to be arranged artistically on the windowsills and studding of our attic room.

The November storm had changed the beach, but the huge cross section of a cedar log that we used for a picnic table was still there. We rejoiced by tap dancing on it.

Frannie carefully rolled up her new slacks and knelt by a tide pool, her bottom in the air and her nose dipped in the water. "There are zillions of little shrimp-like things with fuzzy legs and oodles of hermit crabs." When she got up, she wiped the sand off her knees and said, "Remember when our knees were always dirty and we had to wash them between Saturday night baths?"

We walked on to the point and stopped. The water beyond the low tide line was serene, mirroring a grey sky. Two blue herons stretched long necks in our direction.

"Look! Black fish."

The older members of our family and all the pioneers called them black fish, but in Zoology class I had learned that these huge mammals were Orcas, or killer whales. We stood silently, watching them.

Later as we sat on a log shaking the pebbles out of our shoes, Frannie informed me that she had a new boyfriend named Tyler. "I met him at the USO. He and his friends are from Arkansas. They joined up because they couldn't find jobs in Little Rock. Now they're really stuck. Every Saturday night he comes in from Camp Murray and calls me up. Tyler has two friends who want to come too, and he asked me to get blind dates for them. How about you and your friend Gina?"

I hedged. "Why don't you ask Delaine?"

"She's going steady."

"I don't have the time."

"Robin, you've got to make the time. Did you and Kiko have any dates in high school? Those school mixers don't count as dates. I'll bet you've never been to a party where the kids spin the bottle. Do you even know how to dance?"

"Yes, I do. I learned at Faurots."

"Have you been to the Avalon or the Trianon? Last week, Tyler took me to Parkers'."

"Uncle Tolly let you go to a road house?"

"Don't act so shocked. He didn't know about it. The point is, you need the experience of going out with boys because we'll be getting married in the next five years."

"You, maybe, but not me."

"Yvonne, Delaine's sister, is taking Sociology at the U and she says twenty-three is the average age for getting married. After that, there are more females."

"So what?"

"I'm being realistic. If you think you're going to hold out until you're thirty, you're crazy. When you're thirty, any man the same age will marry someone a lot younger. You'll have to settle for an older man, probably one with kids already."

I felt hot under the collar. "Then I won't get married. I think it's unfair for men to marry women younger than themselves, and those they consider less intelligent. It's as though they have to have the upper hand. It's not going to be that way for me. My husband and I will be equal partners."

Frannie snorted. "You're going to end up an old maid. At least I'm honest about how I feel. You've suppressed all your emotions. You're scared silly, and you'll be sorry. Life is going to pass you by."

"You don't know anything about my feelings, Frannie. You're so boystruck it's pathetic. You're the scared one. If you don't watch out, you'll marry out of desperation and end up bored to death."

I was so angry with Frannie that I lost control of myself and spilled the beans. "I'm in love," I told her. "That's more than you can say for yourself."

"Ye gawds and little fishes!" she exclaimed. "Who is he?"

"Kiko's brother, Tadashi."

Frannie slapped her forehead with the palm of her hand and reeled in a circle as though she would faint. "The family will crucify you. What do you see in him?"

"He's the sweetest person I know. I think he loves me too. But he'll have to wait for me."

"Wait? What do you mean—wait? He'll get tired of waiting for you and marry someone else."

"I can't get married until I'm ready, but I'll know when I'm ready. I don't want to go from my father's house to my husband's without living a life of my own first. Otherwise, I have never belonged to myself, only to them."

Frannie pointed a finger at her head and wiggled it. "I don't know what you're talking about. I think you just want to have fun before you get tied down. You don't know the difference between real love and puppy love."

"What's wrong with wanting to have an adventure or two? I want to do something my grandchildren will approve of, something bizarre, maybe risky, but at least exciting."

"I think getting married is exciting. Wasn't it Katherine Hepburn who talked about the love trap, or was it Jean Arthur in *The Devil and Miss Jones*? With all your fancy aspirations, you got caught in the love trap. I think that's funny."

"Look," I cried, determined to make my point. "If we spend most of our time washing dishes and changing diapers, what do we have to show for it at the end of our lives? Those women in our family history were invisible except for baby and wedding pictures, most of them died young in an epidemic or childbirth, and your mom couldn't dig up their maiden names. It's a conspiracy—herding us into marriage and child raising as though that's all we're good for. Our moms never held jobs, never earned a dime, and they have to beg for money."

Frannie shrugged. "Mom showed me a photo of our parents on a double date. Our mothers were really cute in an old-fashioned way and, believe it or not, our fathers were good-looking too. Your parents were holding hands and my mother was actually flirting with my father."

We walked on to where the tall bluff drops down to an acre or two of lowland covered with big logs, tossed there by high tides. It occurred to me that if I had a boat I could go up-sound and through the Strait of Juan de Fuca to the Pacific Ocean. On the far side of the Pacific wars were being fought. The Japanese had landed in Malaya, the Philippines, and Thailand, and only yesterday they had taken the island of Wake.

Why was I so rebellious? I didn't like what society did to women. But now I had to admit that terrible things were done to men. From the time they were little boys they were being prepared for war, and it had always been that way. Poor Chris.

I followed Frannie as we left the beach, slashing through high grass to the trail that led us over the hill and back to the village. All around us sword fern sprouted out of the ground like green stars. The woods were sodden in December, silently waiting, the ground oozing. Our blind Indian friend, Virgil, had told us that once while walking this trail a cougar had stalked him. He sensed that whenever he stopped so did the cougar.

Two nights after Christmas, I found Mom in a cloud of white tissue paper. On the dining room table was a set of dishes—three platters in different sizes, two vegetable dishes with lids, a gravy boat, and stacks of plates, dessert dishes, and saucers with eight dainty cups.

"Aren't they beautiful?" Mom cried.

I stooped to look. The dishes were translucent and fluted, daintily edged with gold. The flowers painted on them were delicate blue with leaves that were more grey than green and shadows of leaves that were pink.

"Are they Haviland?"

"No, they're Cluny. I bought them from Mrs. McMaster."

I had a vision of the tiny old lady who visited Mom on Sundays and stayed for dinner.

"These were a wedding gift to her mother. Just think. These dishes were brought west on a wagon train during the 1850s before Mrs. McMaster was born. How carefully her mother must have packed them." Mom was beaming. "I bought them for you, Robin. When you get married," and she winked at me, "all these will be yours."

7

On the day Chris enlisted in the Air Corps, Mom went to bed. I found her buried under the covers, curled up in a ball. Her brown hair lay splayed on the pillow. When I begged her to come to dinner, she stirred slightly. "No. Please leave me alone for the time being."

The first thing Dad did when he arrived home from his job as bookkeeper for the city was to remove his oxford-grey coat, which he hung on a chair, and the collar to his white shirt, which he placed on the mantel along with the gold studs that fastened the collar to the shirt. Stripped to his vest with shirtsleeves rolled to his elbows, he was ready to relax with the radio and his pipe. On weekends he put on his overalls to clean ashes out of the furnace or spread tar on the roof to stopper the leaks.

Tonight I found him in the kitchen, wearing Mom's ruffled apron, scrambling eggs. I opened a can of peas and dumped them in a pan. We had to duck under the clothes hung on the lines that crisscrossed the kitchen. Usually mom had the morning's wash cleared away by now. While the eggs and peas cooked, I pulled the clothes down.

I tried to nudge Dad into conversation. "I wonder if Chris was in a parade today. Whenever I go uptown to the dime store on my lunch hour, I see one of those marches."

Dad grunted.

I forged on. "Sometimes there's a Navy or Army band in the lead.

The enlistees are in different colored civvies straggling along—tall, short, husky, even little guys. I suppose they'll all look alike in uniform. People clap for them and wave. I want to cry."

I looked hard at my father with his horn-rimmed glasses. The pores of his Roman nose were enlarged and speckled, as though he had been sprinkled with pepper.

Our kitchen was drab with one window looking out to a latticed porch and the other facing a courtyard for three garages. We had a kitchenette that stored staples, a wood range, an icebox and table. The sink was in a dark corner with a small drainboard on the right-hand side and no cabinetry underneath to hide the soap and dishpan. We had a pantry where our dishes were stored, but we never used the apple box that was attached to the window outside. When we had a big dinner the leftovers were placed on the counter in the pantry, affording us easy access to between-meal snacks.

Dad usually washed the dishes and I dried. He replaced one of the round, iron plates on the stove with a large teakettle for heating the rinse water. As we worked I remembered when I balked at eating parsnips and Dad was scornful of all young people in general and of me in particular. "Kids nowadays love to eat anything that comes out of a can," he'd snort, "or Brussels sprouts at fifteen cents a pound, but the stuff out of Grandpa's garden isn't good enough for them."

He called me "Useless" and "Lazy Bones." I was a bad cook and a poor ornament. When he caught me staring out the window, he'd say, "Come out of your trance, girl. You make me feel like the hen that hatched a duck."

He hated to see me read, play the piano, or paste pictures in my photo album. If Mom were busy in the kitchen, I had to be there even though there was nothing for me to do. I made white sauce for vegetables and dressing for coleslaw, set the table, and filled the sugar bowl from the large container in the kitchenette. During canning season I washed cherries, skinned tomatoes, and stuffed jars with pears and peaches while Mom managed the exigencies of the hot water bath and Dad dallied as supervisor, waiting to pounce on the still-warm jars which he squirreled away in the basement.

I was annoyed by Dad's assumption that I tried all the angles to get out of work. Wasn't my main job to do my homework? Dad would pace the floor when he found me cuddled up with a book. Eventually, I fled to my unheated bedroom to do my homework and wrapped myself up in a blanket. In spite of his interference, I pulled in A's and B's in contrast to Chris' C's and D's. Dad conceded, "She's doing all right—for a girl."

Now that I dragged in, tired and cross after ten hours away from home, he was grudgingly respectful, mindful of my contributions to Mom's cookie jar. After Mom told him that I was privy to military secrets, I heard him say, "She's doing all right—for a girl." That didn't strike me as much of a compliment.

Mom and Dad drove out to Fort Lewis to see Chris and came back with a shopping bag, which I dumped on Chris' bed. I hung up his blue suit and hid his agate ring in the top bureau drawer next to his collections of Indian head pennies and buffalo nickels. I leaned against his highboy thinking about how his voice had changed when he was twelve. For a week Chris could scarcely speak above a whisper; then suddenly, the new bass voice had boomed out of him.

Come to think of it, Chris had waited on me when I was little. He picked me up and carried me home the day I got hurt doing the elephant walk and all the other kids ignored my screams. Another time, when I begged to play cops and robbers with him and his friends, Chris had ignored his pals' protests and said, "Let her play. She isn't hurting anybody." One of the boys shot me with his cap pistol and while I lay dead in the grass, they trooped off to where I was not allowed to go.

Should I be ashamed for complaining so much about having to wait hand and foot on Dad and Chris? No, that wasn't what really bothered me. I resented being expected to serve them as though that was my lot in life, as though I had no right to a life of my own. I was ashamed of being envious of Chris because he was chosen for a college education. Dad had dreamed of Chris the Engineer making his fortune in South America. It wasn't Chris' fault that the war forced him to abandon his schooling two quarters before getting his degree.

I found a note from Chris in my handkerchief box. "Take my bike to Broadway Cycle and trade it for a girl's bike, but be sure to get another Raleigh Gazelle three-speed. They came over in the first shipment of lightweights from England a year or two ago and they're great compared to those balloon-tired jobs made in America. Cheers."

Eventually Mom got out of bed. Thank goodness! I was tired of scrambled eggs and canned vegetables. I gasped when I saw the new refrigerator, the first our family had ever owned.

"Your dad bought the last Coldspot at Sears," Mom announced proudly. "There won't be any more until after the war. From now on, all the factories will be turning out war supplies and we civilians will be on the short end of the stick. We tried to put the icebox in the pantry, but there wasn't room. So, it's on the back porch. We'll store potatoes in it. I'll never get over calling this thing an icebox."

"Now that everybody wants to buy refrigerators, what will happen to the ice man?"

"I guess he'll have to get another job," Mom said as she swung the door open so I could look inside. "We can take out the ice cubes and have room for a quart of ice cream. Won't it be nice having ice cream whenever we want it?" Momentarily, it seemed, Mom had forgotten about Chris.

The Sunday after Mom got out of bed, Tadashi telephoned me. Would I like to go for a walk along Alki Beach?

On the way to Alki, Tadashi entertained me with the Japanese version of the origin of the races.

"Thousands of years ago, before there were humans, before there was a China or a Japan, a magician tried to make humans out of clay and baked

48

them in his oven. The first batch turned out too pale, the second were black as charcoal, but on the third try he baked them just long enough to produce beautiful, golden-brown human beings. And, of course, that's where I come from." He pinched me and I gave him a shove.

"That means that I'm half-baked," I said. "That's the term Dad uses to describe crazy people."

Because of wind and threat of rain, we had the beach all to ourselves. We ran along the water's edge, dodged waves, threw rocks, and chased each other with wet seaweed until we collapsed in the soft sand.

I found a big log that supported my upper back, but Tadashi sat opposite me, his back straight, legs folded in front of him like Buddha.

"How do you do that?" I asked him. "Aren't you uncomfortable?" He shook his head.

Sea lions barked offshore and out among the whitecaps four gulls rode a log. Tadashi pretended to snap a picture of them. "I draw a lot now that the government has taken my camera. I've got an idea for a picture book showing how ridiculous old Japanese customs are. The Issei won't like it much, but I think the Nisei will find it hilarious."

I studied some small shells in my hand and slipped them into my pocket. "Kiko told me they've rounded up more Japanese."

He nodded. "I was at the Atlas Theater last night when they flashed a message on the screen. A couple of old guys were wanted in the lobby. The FBI was waiting for them."

We turned to watch the silver-colored, streamlined ferry, *Kalakala*, chug by on its way to Bremerton.

"The FBI broke up a birthday party thinking that the people were celebrating Pearl Harbor. Last week they took Mr. Ito, chairman of the building committee for our new temple, and five members of his committee. There's no one left who understands the finances. The contractor threatened a lawsuit, demanding $6,000. Nine members had to come up with their own money to pay off the debt. My father was one of them."

Suddenly his eyes dulled as though a light had been switched off. "I'm worried about an anti-Japanese group called the Joint Immigration Committee. They want all the Japanese kicked out of California."

"People like that make me sick!" I exclaimed.

Tadashi reached out and stroked my nose with the back of a finger. "You Hakujin don't have a monopoly on prejudice. I think the most prejudiced people on earth are the Japanese. They've treated the Eta and the Ainu abominably. Their regard for us Japanese-Americans isn't much better. As for the Kibei—the Nisei sent to Japan for a proper education—those I knew begged to come home."

I studied his face, letting shells slip through my fingers and back into the sand. His skin was smooth and bronzed like Kiko's, and both had even and astonishingly white teeth, but their eyes were different. Kiko's were wide without a fold, usually serious and questioning. Tadashi's were tucked neatly at both ends, obliquely, so that he looked impish when he smiled, and they were so black that I couldn't distinguish pupils from iris.

An old man staggered by on the sidewalk above us. "I wonder why he walks like that."

Tadashi's answer was immediate. "He's afraid of falling. That's why he's carrying a cane, which works like a third leg." We watched the old man until he was out of sight.

"Mom says I'm a caution because I've made friends with all the old people in the neighborhood and they tell me their life stories. Mr. Swanberg lives in that bungalow dwarfed by the monkey-puzzle tree. I usually find him sitting on his porch. When he smokes his wife locks him out. He complains about Swedes being called stupid, but he admits to pulling a dumb trick as a young punk fresh over from the old country. He'll tell you he's the guy who almost sank the USS *Minnesota*. He was working in the hold of the ship and caused it to flood. It was already taking on passengers and freight, due to sail to the Orient the next morning."

"Do you suppose that's his only claim to fame?" Tadashi asked.

"Probably. Old folks love to talk about themselves and it doesn't take long for them to get to the nubbin in their lives. Mrs. James lives across the street. She danced with the Prince of Wales when she was young and life has been downhill ever since. She shocks everybody by running around her yard with a cigarette in her mouth."

"So, the highlight of her life was dancing with the Prince? You can't beat that."

"Mr. Ivanoff lives at the end of our block. He told me how he escaped from the Bolsheviks and saw naked corpses hanging like icicles in the railroad stations."

Tadashi grimaced.

"Let me tell you about Mrs. Bryson. She was forced to marry an older man when she was fifteen. When she was twenty, she had four children and the doctor told her that her husband would kill her if she stayed with him. Luckily for her, the husband died in a railroad accident. She is in her eighties now and is still going strong."

"Robin, I'll bet that doctor was the only one who ever stuck up for her. Her family and husband didn't."

"And Mrs. Mangini, our next-door neighbor, came from a small Italian village. Her mother had twelve children; four died in one night of diphtheria and only three lived to adulthood. The mother was a wet nurse. As soon as she had a baby she put it on the cow's teat and then she took a rich person's baby. Mrs. Mangini told her mother that the cow was her real mother."

Tadashi laughed. In a falsetto, he made fun of me. "Mama, you aren't my mama; the cow is my mama. All these elderly friends of yours are immigrants. One of my earliest memories is when Yoshio and I played at the Collins Playfield. The nearby field house was jammed with immigrants. I suppose they were being briefed on how to find jobs and housing. I think that was in 1928, when I was five years old."

We talked about the neighborhoods along Yesler Way, how the Jewish men ate breakfast with their hats on and their sons dressed up like their fathers to go to synagogue.

"Remember how people referred to Garfield High as the League of Nations?" I nodded. "There was such a mix of Asians, Negroes, and

51

Hakujin. It was a great experience. I think it was good even for the rich kids from the Montlake district and Broadmoor who arrived in taxis and limousines. I learned a lot about people on the track team and in photography club. I ignored prejudice and refused to be intimidated. If I expected goodness from people, I got it. Kiko has yet to learn this. The best thing I learned was that happiness comes from within."

"You're a philosopher as well as an artist."

"Aw shucks," he replied, and he hooked his thumbs under his armpits and waved his fingers in a show of mock pride.

What happened next would have shocked my contemporaries and our parents would have been aghast. I've always blurted out my thoughts. They just roll out of my head via my mouth. Mom used to slap me for getting sassy, and Dad lectured me on keeping a partition between my brain and my tongue.

"I love you, Tadashi!" I said without shame or embarrassment.

Tadashi was very quiet for a moment. Only his Adam's apple quivered. He leaned toward me. "You will have a tough time with me, little chickadee. If we had any sense, we would run in opposite directions."

"I don't want to," I said.

"I can't. We'll just have to play it out and see what happens."

We held hands on our way back to the car, Tadashi whistling, "Don't sit under the apple tree with anyone else but me…"

He dropped me off in front of Mrs. Mangini's house. As I stepped off the running board of the car, I heard him say, "I love you too, chickadee. So long."

I watched the Model A Ford go down the hill and disappear. Mrs. Mangini stood on her porch. She beckoned me in. Mrs. Mangini was a widow with a husky voice and hair that frizzed around her face like Einstein's.

"So you've got yourself a boyfriend?" She led me to the kitchen, poured two cups of tea, and pushed a cookie across the table.

"Don't say anything to my mother, please. She would skin me alive if she knew I was seeing him on the sly."

"How old are you, precious?"

"I just turned nineteen."

"You're old enough to do what you want with your life. I left home when I was seventeen. Of all my suitors, I chose the one going to America." She winked at me. "I bought a fancy hat and got sick eating crackers on the boat." Her gravelly voice had degenerated into an asthmatic cough.

She reached her hand across the table and patted mine. "Dearie, have fun with the boyfriends, but be sure to pick a rich man when you marry. Let your head do the choosing."

8

On the last day of 1941, Goldie Mae gathered us in a huddle and announced that we had to work late that night and all of New Year's Day. We were flabbergasted.

Gina puckered her lips in a pout. "But I've got a date!"

"Cancel it. Cancel all your New Year's Eve parties. Phone home and tell your families you'll be late. Now girls, don't get your bowels in an uproar. Once in a blue moon you've a chance to serve your country and this is it."

"Doing what?" we wondered.

"It's hush-hush. I think it's a requisition for building an airfield in Alaska. No one says where. We'll be working on what they call Project A. You'll get time and a half for this. Besides, the boys upstairs collected money for our dinner at one of the best restaurants in town."

It was a day of struggle with words I had never heard before such as humdurgens, concrete busters, carryalls, and angledozers. When we were stuck, Gina and I listened to each other's machines. What were scarifiers? Did he say tandem tows, sumps and flanges? Sometimes the Dictaphone's voice was bedded down in static and we repeated the words and phrases until they got fuzzy.

We didn't have far to go to the restaurant across the street from the Central Building, an old mansion that must have been someone's dream house during pioneer days. Surrounded by a burgeoning city, its front yard became a row of stores on Third Avenue with a pub called the Rathskeller flanking its Marion Street side. To reach the stairs to the Maison Blanc, we had to climb the steep hill almost to the alley.

A dignified waiter ushered us to a large table overhung by a huge chandelier. I found myself sitting between the two older women who had kids. Clara made me feel uncomfortable, but I liked Pat who had been drab looking and down on her luck before she became part of the Dictaphone pool. Goldie Mae changed that. Pat had to wear lipstick and upgrade her hairstyle, go on a diet and buy new clothes. According to what Gina heard, Pat's husband wasn't pleased with all the changes.

The waiter poured me some coffee, all bubbly on top. "Skim off the froth," Goldie Mae said. "That's money."

Our group had never socialized before, but Goldie Mae broke the ice with one of her stories about Prohibition days.

"My Daddy had a still in the woods near our house and the Feds kept pussyfooting around trying to find it. One day they offered me a nickel to show them where Daddy spent his time. I took them down to the creek on a wild goose chase. I was only five years old and smart. I kept the nickel too."

I thought Goldie Mae was the cat's pajamas. Most men hate mouthy women who have opinions of their own, laugh loudly, and yell a lot like Goldie Mae. They would consider her a brassy dame. I liked women who had their say.

We had a wonderful dinner followed by a dessert of ice cream rolled in cocoa and served on a paper doily. Then we went back to work. Skidrigs, batter and plumb piles, go-devils, and stiff-leg derricks. "We can put that on like shooting fish," the Alaska engineer said.

Gina wanted to know what I'd be doing if we hadn't had to work. "I'd be with Kiko. The New Year is a big holiday for the Japanese. The women cook up fancy foods and the men go house-to-house, eating with enameled chopsticks and drinking sake. Grandmother Nakayama taught me how to slice burdock in thin strips. I like Japanese food with one exception; Kazunoko, herring roe on kelp, considered a delicacy, tastes like rubber bands soaked in cod liver oil." Suddenly, it occurred to me that the Japanese probably weren't celebrating much this year.

January was a clutteration of events. I howled when we lost our Saturday half-holiday. When would I see Kiko now that I'd be working a full six-day week?

About the same time, I went from Junior Clerk Steno CAF 2 at $1,440 a year to Assistant Clerk Typist CAF 3 at $1,620.

David Engstrom called to invite me to a celebration at the Swinomish Indian Reservation.

"We're in luck," he said happily. "Anthropology students get to see the real tribal dances. There'll be Puyallup and Muckleshoot from the south, Saanich and Cowichan from British Columbia, and representatives from all tribes in between."

The smokehouse was a thick-beamed, barn-shaped structure with four big fires in the middle of the enclosure. Blue smoke from crackling fir slabs filtered through holes at the peak of the roof. Some Indians ate; others swayed and chanted or stomped and shuddered to the vibrant pounding of drums covered with thin buckskin.

"This is the dance of magic sticks—the Skwedeelitch," David explained. "Tommy Bob has danced three nights trying to deal with his grief. He lost a son at Pearl Harbor."

I studied the beautiful, strong faces of the dancers. I was reminded that Grandpa had played with Indian boys when he was a child. He still used Chinook words he had learned then. When something didn't work, he called it *cultus*. Grandma was his *klootchman* and I was his *tilicum*. Unlike other people, Grandpa never referred to the Indians as *siwashes*.

"Look, the Chief is blackening his face and putting on feathered headgear and a beaded shirt. Now they are getting their spirits!" David cried excitedly. "The Indian Shaker Church is Christian, started by a Squaxin Indian who lived on the Skookumchuck River more than fifty years ago. It's a blend of Catholic, Protestant, and Native American beliefs. Indians say that the power of the shake has saved them from illness and death."

As we drove off the reservation, David and his friends were jubilant. They had seen the Indians catch their spirits and that is what they had come for.

Gina and I finally agreed to blind date the Arkansas boys. It was dark out when we emerged from the Central Building, but I could discern the black Mercury at the curb, Frannie sitting in front with the driver.

Almost immediately two soldiers stepped out and darted in our direction. The good-looking sergeant took one look at Gina and bee-lined for her. Gina looked like a dart had stung her. How did I know it was love at first sight? I knew. But how could it happen so suddenly?

"He sure has her staked out," the other soldier said, apparently as fascinated as I was. "I'm Stonewall Jackson Parish. My friends call me Stony." The accent was soft and southern. He was tall and skinny, red headed and freckled.

After I climbed in next to Frannie and the others settled in the rear seat with Gina in the middle, I met Adrian, the sergeant, and Tyler, who was Frannie's date.

"We've noticed that Seattle girls have long, muscular legs," Tyler said. "Must be from climbing all these hills."

"I'm hungry. Where are we going to eat?" asked Stony.

"How about the Coon Chicken Inn?" was Frannie's suggestion.

What was the matter with Frannie, I thought, suggesting an expensive place like that? I'd heard that privates in the Army were paid only a dollar a day.

"That is beyond the city limits," I informed them. "I know a good restaurant in Chinatown only a few blocks from here."

"How do you know about this restaurant?" Frannie was suspicious. Members of her family never dined out. Uncle Tolly and Aunt Vi couldn't afford it. Mom and Dad had never been to a restaurant that I could remember. But Mr. Nakayama managed to take his family occasionally and even included me. There had to be a difference in our families' approach to life. Was it the Protestant ethic? Going to dinner was an indulgence and they didn't believe in indulging themselves.

"The Golden Pheasant is a Chinese restaurant and the food is wonderful. You get all you can eat for fifty cents."

I could tell by the way they looked at me that none of them had ever been to a Chinese restaurant. Caucasians, as a rule, didn't go to Chinatown unless they were University students on a Sociology field trip.

"You have a great treat in store for you," I assured them.

As we cruised through Chinatown the boys were fascinated with the Chinese signs, the balconies, and the old plank sidewalks fronting buildings on Jackson Street. I told them about the tunnels underneath the buildings, some of which were built on piling or stilts because this area was formerly a tide flat.

When they saw the flophouse signs—25¢ a night—they laughed. "Makes you feel right at home, doesn't it?"

Tyler parked the car on Jackson Street and we walked the half block up the hill on Sixth Avenue to the Golden Pheasant. I was happily hungry as we climbed the stairs under the canopy to the restaurant.

When we were seated, the waiter gave us green menus and pulled the curtains across the entrance to our booth. When the heaping platters arrived, Stony whistled. The food was so good that Frannie called it fan-tas-tic in one sentence and fab-u-lous in another.

With Frannie and Tyler occupied in one corner of the booth and Gina and Adrian in the other, I turned to Stony who sat opposite me and asked him about his life in the Army.

"We've been in the Army since last summer. We couldn't find jobs in Little Rock, so we joined the medical detachment of the 153rd Infantry. It was boring until last week when we went on bivouac to Grays Harbor." He leaned across the table and whispered, "We heard they'd deciphered the Japanese code and expected an invasion."

Stony tried to use chopsticks without success. "When we picked up Frannie her mother was real nice, but her father acted suspicious."

I laughed. "My dad's the same. Before the war, Frannie and I were not allowed to go out with soldiers or sailors. Now that there's a war, servicemen are respectable all of a sudden."

"Your father would rest easier if he knew that whenever I go out with a girl I'm as nervous as a long-tailed cat in a room full of rocking chairs."

"We have to be home by 1:00 a.m."

"No problem. We have to get this borrowed doodlebug back to camp before it turns into a pumpkin. If anything goes wrong, we're AWOL."

The messages in what the menu called fortune cakes were quaint, as though Chinese students unfamiliar with English had dreamed them up. While the others laughed over their fortunes I worried about the ten percent tip, which would be thirty cents, and was relieved when Adrian slipped two quarters under the teapot.

We drove uptown to see *Citizen Kane* at the Palomar. When the boys dropped us off at Frannie's house, Stony stuck his head out the window of the car and called to me, "See you next Saturday night, Sugar."

By the end of January, I was exhausted. I saw David on Friday nights, Stony on Saturdays, and Tadashi Sunday afternoons. The 48-hour week left me little time to sit in my big chair and cogitate.

Wednesdays, I walked uptown after work for my music lesson. From the elevator of the Fischer Studio Building I could hear students running scales and arpeggios, endlessly thumping chords, and some, like the soprano on the top floor, repeating phrases over and over again.

I complained to Mr. Scavenius, expecting sympathy, but he laughed at me. "What if you had to work seven days a week like the defense workers are doing? Men used to work 14-hour days in the mines, and for a pittance too."

"But I have no time to practice. I'm too rushed mornings and too tired at night. What's the use of my coming here each week if I can practice only on Sundays?"

"You practice only fifteen minutes a day if that's all the time you have. Every day you sit down to the piano. It will give you a good feeling and it's worth it."

Before I left, Mr. Scavenius gave me a lecture in that thick Danish accent of his. "This is a very special time of your life. Enjoy it. You lose energy when you are in conflict with yourself."

I vowed not to complain about my busy schedule again. I didn't want to give up anything, certainly not my walks in the park with Tadashi. Feeling sure that I could handle it was like having a kitten in my pocket.

9

I was disgusted when I saw the white sandbags, trimmed in red, piled at the entrance to Best's Apparel.

"It's a booth for selling war bonds," Gina explained.

"Why do women dress up grim realities?" I wondered. "I hate to see them strutting down the street in uniform wearing those REMEMBER PEARL HARBOR buttons."

Gina nodded her disapproval. "What do you think of mothers who tell reporters that they wish they had ten more sons to give or girlfriends and wives saying, 'I'm glad he died that way'?"

During the first gloomy weeks of the war I had expected that rigid regulations would transform our daily lives, but the government continued to conduct business in a democratic manner as much as a government can do during wartime. I had fears of becoming a slave to my job, but workers quit without being caught by freezing orders and promotions went through as usual.

It was a shock then to see Kiko's scrapbook. She had methodically searched through the *Seattle Star*, the *Times*, and the *Post-Intelligencer* for articles about Japanese- Americans and included in her clippings were cartoons that pictured them, as well as the enemy Japanese, with toothy, malevolent grins, and letters to the editor, which were hateful and patronizing. The solution to the Japanese problem, according to many, was to ship them inland away from the West Coast.

"We're going to be evacuated," Kiko announced.

"You're kidding!" I cried.

"Tad, Yoshio, and I attended one of the Tolan hearings. Only two people spoke in our favor. We heard people say, 'Get rid of the Japs and we'll have more land'."

"Does this affect both aliens and citizens?"

"That's right. Count everyone on the West Coast and it will amount to 120,000 people."

"Do you mean that your grandmother and Yuki would have to go? That's crazy."

Kiko's eyes flashed with fire. "Grandmother and Yuki might bomb Boeing Aircraft. Mayor Millikin said that we could burn down the city, signal enemy submarines, set fire to forests, and dynamite Grand Coulee Dam."

I leafed through more of the clippings. There were obnoxious columns written by Henry McLemore and Westbrook Pegler. One article told of a man dragging a school patrol boy from his post because he was Japanese. The boy had been born in the United States and was a citizen. The man was not.

One hundred swastika pins were seized. If the Japanese Army invaded Seattle these pins could be used to identify fifth columnists, the agents said. I exploded. "Even I know that the swastika is an ancient Hindu and Buddhist symbol and that the Nazi version is a reversal of the Buddhist one. How come they're so dumb?"

When Tadashi came home, I asked him if he thought there would be an evacuation.

"Yes, they're talking about it. I'd be for moving east right now and getting settled somewhere else, but where? Nine governors filed protests. They don't want their states to be dumping grounds for Japanese. Even the universities don't want us."

On the 19th of February, President Roosevelt signed Executive Order

#9066, giving the Secretary of War the power to exclude people thought to be dangerous to national security.

I rushed to the Nakayama house after work only to find that Kiko and Tadashi were not at home. Mr. Nakayama motioned me in.

"I'm sorry about the evacuation," I said, feeling that whatever I said was inadequate.

His grin faded. "I thought I gotta show Tadashi and Akiko how to run hotel if I go. We all go."

"What will you do with the hotel?"

"Sell everything. People want bargains. Maybe we put little in bank."

"Oh, Mr. Nakayama, must you sell the hotel? Couldn't you board it up for now? I've just gotten a raise. I pay my mother $35 a month room and board. I don't need much for expenses. Maybe I can help with taxes or whatever payments you have to make."

"I don't own hotel. I lease. Furniture and equipment mine."

"You couldn't store it?" He shook his head.

"Your house? What about this house?"

Mr. Nakayama cleared his throat, but his voice came out more scratchy than usual. "We rent house." He patted my shoulder. "You good friend. It gonna be hard for Japanese."

Going home on the bus, I felt shredded by conflicting emotions. I hadn't thought twice about offering my college money, but it wasn't enough and that saddened me and made me angry and embarrassed. Had I been presumptuous to offer money to Mr. Nakayama and query him about his finances? Mom and Dad would think so.

To make matters worse, Uncle Fritz had stayed for supper.

"Sorry I'm late," I said breathlessly as I washed my hands at the kitchen sink. In a big pan on the table was one of my favorite dinners—pork backs and necks simmered all afternoon in sauerkraut. I loved to pick the whitish marrow out of the bones.

Uncle Fritz was telling a story about two men digging a well. "The man on top, pulling up the pails, was a practical joker. He told the man thirty feet down that he had to go to the house, but instead, he took the bell off a blind horse and shook it near the top of the well, stomping as though he were a horse shaking off flies. The man in the well shouted, 'Whoa, Blaze!' From that day on, everybody yelled 'Whoa, Blaze!' at this man until he was old and childish." Uncle Fritz threw back his head and laughed.

I didn't laugh. What was funny about being stuck thirty feet down a well, afraid that a horse might land on you?

Uncle Fritz pointed at a little package next to my plate. I pulled off the tissue paper. Inside was a ceramic owl pin. "I like it, Uncle Fritz. I will wear it to work tomorrow," and I held it under my chin against my white blouse.

"How is your friend?"

"She wasn't at home."

"It's going to be hard for you having her go away, but it's best for her."

Just how was it best for Kiko to be uprooted from her home and school, I wanted to say, but I remained silent.

"A lot of hotheads could make it unpleasant for the Japs."

My dresser drawers brimmed with scarves and pretty things Uncle Fritz had given me. In return, did I have to agree with him on everything?

"Who'll run the farms while they are gone?"

"The Filipinos."

"It's going to cost millions to evacuate the Japanese."

"Yes, it will, but it's a military necessity. We have to eliminate the possibility of sabotage and espionage. There's been radio communication with enemy submarines along the coast. The Japs can support this country by submitting cheerfully. We all must make sacrifices for the war effort."

"Why haven't German and Italian aliens been jailed?"

"Some are being rounded up."

"You and Dad are sons of German immigrants. Why isn't the FBI checking you out?"

"We're citizens."

"Kiko and Tadashi are citizens."

Uncle Fritz laughed. "I'm going to re-name you 'Miss Why,' young lady. Don't you know that more Germans have settled this country than any other ethnic group? We've helped in a big way to make the United States what it is today. This is white man's country. Other races are here strictly on tolerance."

That made me mad. I wanted to say: "I suppose Negroes are tolerated because their ancestors were brought here against their will. Asians are tolerated because they offered cheap labor for building railroads and risked their lives in the mines. And women in this white man's country are tolerated because without us there'd be no future generations."

For once, I didn't let my thoughts spill out, but they knew I was holding back when I said, "I don't agree with you, Uncle Fritz."

Mom fidgeted and Dad frowned. "Why can't you discuss anything without flying off the handle?" Dad addressed me, not Uncle Fritz.

The phone rang and I ran to answer it.

"I'm sorry I missed you." Kiko's voice was clear but tiny, as though she were sitting in my ear. "My father is having a dreadful time with my mother and grandmother. They are terrified. They think we will be taken away to be killed."

10

Tadashi and I had started our Sunday walk through the Arboretum. "We're going to be prisoners of our own government, condemned without a trial and herded like sheep into the camps because we are law-abiding."

I tried to be reassuring. "Each new wave of immigrants has experienced prejudice—the Swedes, the Irish, the Italians. They've all been through it."

"But Europeans were allowed to own land. The immigrants from Japan weren't. Did you know that there are laws forbidding intermarriage? Anti-miscegenation laws? In fact, if a Nisei woman marries a man from Japan, she loses her U.S. citizenship."

We plunged into the murk of heavy fog. I pulled on my bandanna and pushed my hands into the deep pockets of my jacket.

It was Tadashi who changed the subject. "Remember when Garfield produced Sigmund Romberg's *Desert Song* and the girls swooned over Hiram Derby because of his beautiful voice? Did you get a crush on him too?"

"Yes, I did, but I got over him fast the next Monday morning in Civics class. It was disillusioning to see him out of costume, doodling on his white cords with a fountain pen."

Out on the Sound, foghorns resonantly proclaimed the presence of big ships: *BE-WARE, BE-WARE.* Little boats tooted. Eerie wisps of mist, caught by gusts of wind, rolled along the ground like ghosts of children playing.

"This is like Alaska," Tadashi remarked. "I spent two summers in the canneries, hired for three months at $50 a month, and missed my graduation last year because of an early departure. When the *Otsego*, which was a German raider during World War I, reached Unimak Pass in the Aleutians a one-hundred-mile gale caused waves to crash over the bow, hitting staterooms on the upper deck."

Tadashi's eyes widened. "The Bering Sea was a glorious green and white marble, so vast, strange, and lonely. The goonies and porpoises followed us and once we spotted a sailing ship and whales. It was day all the time up there. We worked around the clock and slept only when there was a lull in the catch. Out on the bay a hundred boats with grey or white sails plied back and forth with men pulling on their nets. When the big run hit the scow brought in 600,000 salmon and the sorters stood with gaff hooks in both hands, separating humpback, king, dog, and sockeye at two hundred a minute."

"I wish I could have an experience like that."

He looked at me more amused than amazed. "Would you want to be dirty for weeks at a time, eating terrible food, never getting enough sleep? When we left there, the *Otsego* was so overloaded with canned salmon that it was below water line, and we hit a rock and had to send out an SOS to the Coast Guard. That was scary. One minute in that water and you're dead."

"It would be exciting to work in Alaska."

"Coming back they had me on the black gang, passing coal to the engines and hoisting ashes overboard. We Orientals were crowded in steerage with the salmon heads and tails that were saved for fertilizer. My mother burned my clothes when I got home and it took weeks to get that awful smell out of my nose. You still want to be an Alaska boy?"

"Yes, it would be an adventure. Women never have interesting adventures. I want my grandchildren to approve of me."

"Doing what, for instance?"

I couldn't think of a thing. Feeling embarrassed, I said weakly, "Like working on a tugboat maybe, or being a deckhand on a ferry."

"You consider those adventures?"

"It would be more fun than pounding a typewriter all day."

"I think you want to do something all by yourself to prove your worth. Just being alive is an adventure. Getting married is an adventure. Remember: An adventure wrongly considered is an inconvenience. An inconvenience rightly considered is an adventure."

An eagle broke through the fog bank, saw us and veered skyward. It was a sign. Tadashi pulled me close and kissed me. After a long, first kiss, I nuzzled his jacket. "You make me feel woozy," I said breathlessly.

He started to shake and when I looked up at him, he was laughing. "You make me feel woozy too," he said and he hugged me all the way back to the car.

The following weekend the Nakayamas invited me to go with them for their last visit to the farm. I had gone there many times, usually in Uncle Daisho's truck, since Mr. Nakayama refused to own a telephone or an automobile. After all the fuss about Tadashi's buying a white elephant, here was Mr. Nakayama actually riding in the Model A. At least it saved Uncle Daisho a trip from Kent valley and another to take us home again.

When we arrived at the white, two-storey house surrounded by huge maples, Uncle Daisho and Aunt Kazzie greeted us. The four cousins who were closest to Yuki's age were about to spirit her away when their father warned them, "Don't go now. We eat."

Almost immediately we sat down at the large kitchen table and Aunt Kazzie filled bowls with udon—delicious noodles and broth decorated with slices of pink and white fish cake, wedges of hard-boiled eggs, green onions, spinach and bits of chicken. There was no silverware on Aunt Kazzie's table. Everyone fished out the noodles with chopsticks, biting off a comfortable amount and letting the extra fall back into the bowl. After the solids were eaten, the bowl was raised to the lips and the broth slurped, often noisily. It was fun to eat this way.

The deep soup bowls with their delicately painted bamboo branches contrasted with the simplicity of the kitchen. My eyes roamed over the worn and faded linoleum, unpainted cabinets, the large sink that had a slanting drainboard on one side and an old table on the other. The single faucet had to be pumped to bring water from the well. I had seen Uncle Daisho use a shoulder yoke to bring pails of water inside to fill the reservoir on the back of the wood stove.

It always surprised me to see the women rush to serve the men and boys first, then me, before they sat down. They kept one eye on the males, ready to hop up to offer more soup, fill a teacup, or look for an ashtray if one was needed. The men never had to ask. What was amazing was Kiko's acceptance of this custom.

During lunch, Mr. Nakayama and Uncle Daisho talked loudly and angrily in Japanese. The women looked alarmed and the five children watched their elders with astonishment caught in the jet black of their eyes. Tadashi flashed a half smile of reassurance to me.

When I hurried outside to the porch swing, he followed me. "My uncle is preparing the earth for planting. My father says he's crazy. Someone else will benefit from his hard work. But Uncle Daisho is determined to do it. He doesn't want to face the fact that he is going to lose his land. The farm is in his eldest son's name and he will be unable to make payments during internment. He has no money saved. One doesn't get rich selling vegetables at the Pike Place Market."

When Kiko appeared, she sat down beside me. "My brother isn't telling you that the government has threatened Japanese farmers. They have to seed and cultivate their lands for the sake of production. So how do they buy seed when their assets are frozen? And how do they find buyers for their property if they must work up to the last day?"

"The government should put Japanese assets in trust until the war is over," I said, and I was convinced this was the answer to the problem.

"They won't. Some Hakujin will get Uncle Daisho's farm."

I felt stabbed by Kiko's bitterness. Again my eyes met Tadashi's. His half-smile seemed one of apology.

"Some people will profit from the Japanese evacuation; some will profit from the war. That's life." Tadashi said.

"Wars are for profit," Kiko spouted.

Tadashi frowned. "Everyone is involved in causing wars."

"Don't include me," Kiko snapped. "I didn't have anything to do with this one. It won't make me rich."

Tadashi gave her a brotherly pat and murmured, "Shikata ga nai."

I had heard that expression before. It meant, "It can't be helped."

When Uncle Daisho called Tadashi away, Kiko and I walked the path between the cornfield and cabbage patch to our favorite spot along the Green River.

"How can I possibly stuff all my things in one sea bag? That's what they say we can take. What will I do with my books and photo albums?"

"Store them at my house. We have five bedrooms and the room at the head of the stairs is empty most of the time. I'm sure Mom wouldn't mind your using it for the duration. I'll ask Dad about the extra garage. It's only a lean-to with a dirt floor, but Tadashi could use it for his car."

I looked down, afraid that my face might betray my anxiety. I knew that Mom would stonewall the idea. "What if they don't come back and we're stuck with all that stuff? What if it collects moths? What if our storing their things gets us in trouble with the government?" I would be at Mom's mercy. I would have to be grateful for the use of this empty room in my parents' house. I would suffer the proper amount of humiliation before Mom would relent. Abject. That was the word. I would have to be abject.

As for Dad, until recently he had rented the garage for $2 a month and he'd be glad to get $24 for the full year. I'd let him think it was Tadashi's money, not mine.

"I'm lucky to have you, Robin. Lots of our friends have destroyed their treasures, antiques, and art objects. Perhaps it's better to destroy things than to give them away. People come into the stores on Jackson Street and say, 'I'll give you a dollar for this and a dollar for that.' They never think about paying a fair price. And it isn't just the Hakujin, Robin. Suzi and her boyfriend went to dinner at a Chinese restaurant and the waiters let them sit. They've been going to that place for years. It was humiliating."

We stopped to lean on a weathered, snake fence, its rough cedar slabs crisscrossed so the fence stood without nails or posts. Behind us The Mountain loomed from the valley floor, a daytime ghost in a purple haze. The March wind jerked at our coat collars and high above us two kites zigzagged across the cloudy sky. When we reached the river, we sat down on the bank. Kiko pulled up a long piece of grass and chewed its tender end.

"It's hard on the Issei because so many of them can't speak English. They don't understand what is going on and don't know what to do. It's hard on those who lost their jobs; especially hard on women who've never worked whose husbands have been taken away. A photographer friend of my father had all his equipment confiscated. They took him away and left his wife destitute. The government has taken the professionals, those who could have been of help to the Issei."

Kiko handed me clippings from her pocket. She had underlined what one congressman had said, "I'm for catching every Japanese in America, Alaska and Hawaii now and putting them in concentration camps. Damn them. Let's get rid of them now." General DeWitt said, "The Japanese is an enemy race."

"Two-thirds of us are citizens of the United States. We aren't in favor of what the Japanese military is doing and neither are most of the people in Japan. My cousins in Japan will go hungry before this war is over."

"Any news about your Uncle Shig?"

"He's in a camp in Montana." Kiko bent toward me as though she wanted to impart a secret. "There were over fifty Japanese men rounded up and jailed in the first twenty-four hours after Pearl Harbor, mostly professionals. So you see, they had a list."

I nodded. "Our government was preparing for war."

"Prejudice makes your heart and spirit shrivel inside. No matter how hard I try to reassure myself, I wonder if I really belong to an inferior branch of the human race."

"I think I know how you feel," I hastened to say. "Sometimes I feel that way because I am a woman."

There were tears on Kiko's cheeks. "And I am both woman and Japanese. Tad calls me a rebel. All that feistiness is my way of waging war with myself, trying to feel that I am worth something, that I'm as smart as anybody else."

It started to rain, but we didn't move. Large drops splattered on our faces and dripped off our chins. When we heard the clanging of the triangle on the back porch, we got up and started back to the house.

Hanako was barking at the foot of a big maple. Yuki and her cousins were in the tree house.

Kiko hung her head. "We had to come today because they are talking about a curfew. We'll be confined to our houses from 8:00 p.m. to 6:00 a.m., and we have to remain within five miles of our homes. I've known this place all my life. I may never see Uncle Daisho's farm again."

On March 30th, Mom brought the newspaper to the kitchen for me to read while we ate dinner.

"There were 237 Japanese from Bainbridge Island taken to the train today, headed to Manzanar in California. They call it a test run."

I gasped as I read the article. "They gave those people only one week to dispose of their belongings. What would we do if we had only one week to get rid of all our stuff?"

"When will Kiko's family be leaving?"

"The end of April, I think. Did you see this about the Filipino and his Japanese wife? That couple will be separated for the duration of the war because the government refuses to let the husband accompany his wife to camp and they won't let her remain behind."

I threw the paper down in disgust. "The women and children are tagged like cattle, herded by young soldiers with bayonets. Spies, my foot! Strawberry farmers. Poor people who have worked hard all their lives."

Mom spoke after a long pause. "Fiddlesticks! This is wartime, Robin. I'm sure the government and the President know what is best."

Dad had stopped in the doorway to listen in. "Don't let your bleeding heart run off with your bloody head," he warned, before he ducked out.

11

In April 1942, the cherry tree in our backyard looked like a beautiful woman gussied up with white jewelry. I wondered how the daffodils, camellias, and rhodies could bloom so profusely while a terrible war was being fought all over the world.

In April, all my friends moved away.

First, it was Bessie Capeloto who had immigrated to Seattle in the late twenties from the Isle of Rhodes. I guess I taught Bessie a lot of English. We played cops and robbers and as pirates we pricked our fingers to write our names in blood. We were proud of the note line between our houses; two lines of string, which transported notes, popcorn, and candy bars.

I was upset when Bessie announced that she was getting married. "I didn't know you were going with anyone."

Bessie arched her beautifully plucked brows. "I met him last summer while we were in California. Our families come from the same village."

"But you hardly know him. Is your father pushing you to marry him? You're in the United States now. You can marry whomever you choose."

Bessie shrugged. "I like him a lot," and her eyes got misty.

Later in the week, when I delivered a wedding present, Bessie showed me her bedroom. The walls were covered from floor to ceiling with comforters, bedspreads, sheets, towels, and table linen. Card tables were set up for kitchen things.

As I prepared to leave, Mr. Capeloto cut me off at the front door. I had never paid much attention to him, but now, coming face to face with him, I was fascinated by how different he looked close up. His eyes were sharp though the left one wandered a bit. A snappy little mustache gave him a cocky air. He probably hadn't had much education, but he seemed smart enough. He was a small man, a bantam rooster married to a big hen. Mrs. Capeloto, like Mrs. Nakayama, had not bothered to learn English.

"You tell your father that he's dead wrong about the Nazis. I heard a man from Poland last night, at the synagogue, tell about the cattle cars taking Jews away from their homes to God knows where. He saw a woman beg a bystander to take her baby. He took it and threw it into the next car."

"He threw the baby?" A little movie screen inside my head showed the face of the mother as she gave the baby away. I tried to turn the movie off, but it kept on going. I looked into the face of the bystander as he threw the baby. The camera switched to the woman as she collapsed.

"Well, now, I didn't mean to make you cry. I just want you to tell your father that what we hear isn't propaganda," and he stalked off.

Mom and I were the only gentiles at the wedding. We were ushered to a portion of the building reserved for women. We were the only ones who sat still through the long ceremony. Everyone else jumped up and moved about and visited with each other while Bessie and her tall groom stood under the Chupa.

"They look like lambs led to slaughter," Mom whispered.

When the couple drank the wine and the groom smashed the glass under his heel, the wedding was over.

Later, as I looked out my bedroom window at Bessie's house, I knew I probably wouldn't see her again. I felt bereft. It seemed like only yesterday that we climbed the holly tree to its second-storey room and played pirates under the front porch.

The next person to leave was David Engstrom, destined for a conscientious objectors' camp in Oregon. After the trip to the Indian reservation, he had taken me to dinner at the Commons on campus and to the Showboat and Penthouse theaters. He sent me poetry, magazines, papers, clippings, letters, and a book or two. I dumped everything in a basket to read later.

"I don't know how he does it," Mom said, "but he manages to hit both morning and afternoon mail deliveries."

On the day David came to say goodbye, I returned home to find him sitting in Dad's chair. "I wrote a term paper about Seattle's Hooverville," he was telling Dad. "It was one of the largest in the country and covered nine acres. I talked to a couple who lived in a tiny trailer and a man who slept on the ground under a rowboat."

While I helped Mom prepare coffee and cinnamon rolls, she grumbled. "Why do you run off and leave your father and me to entertain your boyfriends? We don't have time for such foolishness. He sure is a talker—a real stick-in-the-mud."

I cringed. I wished Mom would wait until guests were gone before commenting on them.

David related his experiences helping a census taker. "Little Boston is an Indian colony on a spit in Puget Sound with about a hundred Indians living in shacks made out of driftwood."

After consuming a cinnamon roll, David continued. "Those backwoods are full of Silvershirts. They don't want the government to know they're there. One old bird refused outright to give any information about himself—said he had no faith in the government."

David turned to me. "I've been reading about the Civil War. If Lincoln was such a visionary, why didn't he let the southern states secede? Was saving the Union more important than saving all those lives?"

He made me promise to write him once a week. "It's going to be lonely down there. I'm assigned to Wyeth Station near Hood River, Oregon, and I have to be there tomorrow. I wish I were going to a camp near a university."

When he left, he shook hands with me and called me kitten. "I'll be back, kitten."

A few days later, Goldie Mae caught me in the lobby on my way in. "Don't take off your coat. We're going to the County-City Building. Gina and Adrian are getting married this morning and we are to be witnesses."

"They've known each other only three months."

"Stop grumbling, Robin. Hell's bells, you may do the same thing some day."

We found Gina and Adrian outside the judge's chamber. Gina took me aside. "Adrian has been transferred to another outfit. I'm taking a leave of absence so I can follow him." She was breathless, excited.

When we went in for the wedding, old Judge Claypool lectured the bride and groom: "Cross-stitch the motto: Shut Up. Frame it and hang it on the wall. Those words are sacred; they've saved many a marriage."

When Gina left for Wilmington, North Carolina, I was the only one to see her off. King Street Station was jammed with GIs carrying barracks bags, red caps, and young women with small children. "When I get back, I hope I get the desk next to yours, Robin," Gina said before the crowd swallowed her.

I stood next to the firebox of the hissing locomotive. After the shrill whistle and the "*All Aboard*," the powerful arms began to drive the wheels and steam exploded out of the stack in mighty chuff-chuffs. When the train began to move, I chased it to the end of the platform. I wanted to be on that train.

On their next visit, Stony and Tyler tried to tell us that they were shipping out.

Frannie quipped: "Loose lips sink ships."

After dinner in Chinatown, we drove to Volunteer Park and climbed the water tower. As we neared the top, Stony gasped, "I feel like I've been rode hard and put away wet."

On the way down, the boys bantered and shoved each other. Stony said, "You spit in the churn that time, old bud." Tyler replied: "You're a pal spelled R-A-T. You aren't worth diddley-squat."

When I heard Stony say, "It don't matter none," I wondered if he was trying to be funny or was that part of his lingo?

As we emerged from the water tower, Frannie and Tyler took off on a walk around the reservoir and I led Stony beyond the conservatory to the graveyard where Princess Angeline, daughter of Chief Seattle, is buried.

Obviously, Stony was not interested in Seattle history. He leaned against a tombstone under a blossoming cherry tree. "Adrian's been transferred to another outfit, probably because they need a sergeant and he's headed for a port of embarkation. He'll end up in Africa or Europe in the middle of the fighting somewhere. I think Tyler and I are bound for Alaska."

Adrian had said that Stony would never see thirty because he was such a daredevil. Once, he'd hung on to the edge of a trestle while a dozen box cars rumbled over him. He didn't look dare-devilish to me. His face was pale, his freckles bleached out. It was as though his youth was being sucked out of him.

"I'm a lousy soldier. I don't like having no control over my life."

We threaded our way between the tombstones to a path. "You and Frannie are different. I get the feeling that she is searching for a man in her life. I don't pick up the same feeling about you."

"Frannie is boy-crazy and always has been. The family has named her the 'streamlined kid.'"

"But you. What about you?"

I had never talked about Tadashi to anyone, not even to Goldie Mae. I hesitated before I spoke. "My best friend's twin brother is someone I like a lot."

"I have a girlfriend at home, but I don't think she'll wait for me."

"My friends are being evacuated from the West Coast because they are Japanese-Americans."

Stony whistled. "Whoa. Don't you know better than to complicate your life like that? If you married him, people would make your life miserable." He stopped and faced me. "Don't get your dander up, Robin. Your eyes go black when you get mad. I just don't want to see you get hurt."

"Think of it, 120,000 people are being moved inland—old ladies, babies, children. Two-thirds of them are American citizens. Three-fourths are under twenty years of age."

"No kidding. Sounds like they're getting a bum rap."

At evening's end, Stony saw me to my door, grabbed me and kissed me.

"I've wanted to do that for a long time," he said as he backed down the stairs. "So long, Sugar."

The Nakayamas were the last to go. Kiko said that her father had to report to a Civil Control Station to register the family. "And all of us have to see a doctor. Can you imagine my mother and grandmother going to a Hakujin for a medical exam?" She laughed and made a face. "We'll be limited to what we can carry: responsible for our own bedding, toilet articles, extra clothes, and eating utensils. It's ridiculous to expect Grandmother and Yuki to carry all their essentials themselves."

When Tadashi brought the first load of boxes to my house, he drove all the way to the back porch and unloaded hastily; then he and Kiko took the boxes upstairs. After the job was done, they left immediately for home. One evening they made three trips, hurrying because of the 8:00 p.m. curfew.

When Tadashi brought the car, Kiko and I sat on the back steps while he drove it into the garage. When he came out, after a long interval, he padlocked the doors and handed the keys to me.

"If you need to use the car, get somebody to install the battery."

"I don't know how to drive."

"Learn, then."

"Dad wouldn't let me without insurance."

"You could have a lot of fun with a car."

I wondered why boys were so crazy about cars, but I was glad that Tadashi trusted me with his Model A.

On my way to bed, I looked into the small room at the head of the stairs. I knew Mrs. Nakayama's sewing machine and good dishes were stored there, with the butsudan and embroidered screen, Kiko's books and albums, and Tadashi's drawings.

I stopped by to see the Nakayamas on the night before the evacuation. I felt sadness beyond tears as I stood in the empty house. The stove was gone and it was cold. The only remaining bed was reserved for Grandmother. Everyone else would sleep on the floor. Tadashi was sitting on his blanket reading by a naked light bulb in the ceiling. Kiko and I leaned against the wall because there were no chairs. Mr. and Mrs. Nakayama sat on the window seat in the dining room.

"It isn't going to be much fun tonight. We have only enough food for breakfast."

Kiko seemed unusually agitated when she and Tadashi walked me to the bus stop. "None of us could take Yuki's dog to the vet today to have her put to sleep. We've dreaded this for weeks. But we can't leave her behind without making some provision for her. Robin, this is a lot to ask, but could you take her for us?"

"I'll take her home with me and keep her until Yuki comes back."

Kiko began to cry.

"Are you sure your folks won't mind?" Tadashi asked.

"How could Mom and Dad refuse me Hanako? I've never had a dog."

I saw their faces relax, but mine stiffened with apprehension. Would I be allowed to keep the dog?

I set the alarm for the next morning and by 7:00 a.m. was walking down Yesler Way to Collins Playfield and the Buddhist Temple. A dozen Army trucks and buses lined the north side of the street while soldiers paced the area. Roughly two hundred people milled around, and suitcases and bags of every description were piled on the sidewalk.

When I found the Nakayama family, Grandmother and her canary held center stage. Mr. Nakayama conversed with his mother in Japanese, apparently trying to persuade her to leave the bird behind, but she stood her ground, expressionless as a statue.

"She won't go without the bird," Mr. Nakayama told the young soldier who blocked their way.

Finally, the soldier shrugged and directed them to board the bus. The old lady struggled on with Tadashi's help, and then he helped his mother aboard, carrying the birdcage and all their baggage himself.

Yuki sat on the curb with the dog on her lap. When her father leaned over her, she did not look up. Suddenly she jumped up, ran to me with the leash, then with tears streaming down her face, she dashed to the bus, leaving Hanako straining in a mighty effort to follow her.

"Goodbye, Robin," Mr. Nakayama said, and he shook hands with me. "Nice of you to see us off."

Kiko broke down. "This is the end of everything for me—my scholarship, my education, my career as a social worker. Everything's done for."

I squeezed her. "We'll go to school together after the war. Maybe I'll be a social worker too. This won't last forever."

"You dreamer you," Kiko exclaimed. "This is going to be a long war, Robin. It's humiliating being carted away like we were criminals." We hugged briefly, and then Kiko swung the strap of her purse over her left shoulder and walked to the bus where she collected her big suitcase before disappearing inside.

I found Tadashi kneeling beside me, petting the dog. We reached for each other. He gripped me firmly around the waist and stooped to press his cheek against mine. Mom had always warned me about showing affection in public. I threw that admonition to the winds. With the crowd milling around us, no one was concerned about our tearful farewell, and I wasn't concerned either. We were alone in a forest.

"Don't take it so hard, Robin. Maybe we can turn this inconvenience into an adventure."

Someone shouted through a bullhorn.

"Take good care of yourself, little chickadee," Tadashi murmured. Then he picked up a mesh bag bulging with paperbacks, tossed a large suitcase into one of the trucks, and nodded at me as he swung himself onto the bus.

After the doors were shut, the buses continued to sit. "This is ridiculous," I heard myself say.

"This is criminal!" exclaimed a middle-aged woman. "Two of my most promising piano students are being evacuated. This isn't happening to Hawaiian Japanese. I know. I have friends in Hawaii."

When the motors of the buses and trucks started up, the small group on the sidewalk waved goodbye, and the soldiers, guns in hand, jumped onto the Army trucks as the procession moved toward Rainier Avenue.

The newspaperman with the camera disappeared. So did the piano teacher. Hanako and I stood alone and watched the convoy until it was out of sight.

12

I fell in love with Hanako on the way home, amazed at the way she trotted along, instantly responsive to each small tug on the leash. Head bent low, tail at half-mast, this little fox terrier walked into her future obediently and with dignity.

I've seen the full spectrum of emotions displayed on dogs' faces: anticipation, disappointment, joy, love, fear, and grief. Hanako was grieving.

When I opened the door to the living room, Mom stood, hands on hips, with an accusatory look. "What have we here?"

"It's Hanako, Yuki's dog. I want to keep her for Yuki."

"Be sensible, Robin. You're gone ten hours a day, six days a week. How can you possibly care for a dog?"

"I'll walk her first thing in the morning and again at night. You would have to care for her while I'm gone. If you feel that you can't do it, let me know and I'll make other arrangements, but I'm not going to let this little dog die."

I knew at that moment that if Mom decided against keeping the dog, I would move out. It was a frightening prospect. The Depression had led me to believe that I could never make it on my own. But Goldie Mae would see that I did, even to finding me an apartment.

At bedtime, I made a nest in my big chair for Hanako. As I stroked her under the chin and gently squeezed her ears, she responded by looking straight at me with sad eyes. When I snuggled under the covers, Hanako jumped out of the chair and onto the bed. Overwhelmed by tender feelings for this warm little body, I finally let go the tears I'd held back all day.

At breakfast the next morning, Mom sighed. "She's an old dog. Look at the white in her muzzle." The look of resignation on Mom's face was a good sign.

But she made me suffer nevertheless. "Your dog pee-daddled behind the kitchen stove. You'd better clean it up because I'm not going to." Or, she complained, "This dog is shedding. We've got hair on everything."

Hanako perked up after a week or two. When I came home from work, she greeted me with yippy barks and joyful wiggles. I threw off my coat and rolled on the floor with her, and miraculously, the tug of war in my chest loosened and the ache in my eyes eased. Hanako gave me a joy I had never experienced before. Mom didn't let on that she liked the dog, but she did. When she sat on the davenport embroidering, Hanako cozied close with her chin on Mom's knee.

In the meantime, Dad volunteered for Civil Defense and was given a ration card for food and gasoline to be used only in an emergency. After an attack warning there would be a freeze order prohibiting the sale of all consumer commodities, he said. Everyone should have a half-tank of gasoline at all times.

Dad and Uncle Fritz agreed that some of the plans that the government had come up with for evacuating the City were ridiculous. How could children, old people, and sick patients be moved, and to where? It had been mentioned that in case of an invasion, the Army could fall behind the Cascade Mountains and use them as a line of defense. Uncle Fritz constantly bemoaned the war news, such as the surrender of 100,000 troops by a Dutch commander, giving the Japanese control of Java.

"Something terrible happened in Alaska the first week of June," I told them. "Colonel Talley, the Head Engineer in Alaska, tried to tell our Colonel Goertz about it, but the censor broke in and stopped them."

It would have been nice if Dad and Uncle Fritz had shown a little interest. After all, I was the only person in the family working for the War Department. They ignored me. Was it because I was only nineteen and a girl? Or did they feel threatened by my growing independence? Uncle Fritz repeatedly reminded me that when the war ended and "our boys" returned, I'd be out of a job and would have to become a full-time wife and mother.

Mid-June, Frannie and I moved to Indianola for the summer. It would be different this year because we had jobs and would have to get up before five to make the 6:10 a.m. ferry, eat dinner at 7:00 p.m., and bed down by 9:00 p.m. Mom and Aunt Vi warned us that Grandma was not to get our breakfast or oversee our lunch making.

During the evenings on these longest-of-the-year days, we tramped the woods or beach with Hanako in the lead. The Indian women were back; stuffing gunnysacks with fat fish they found under rocks and called "honkers." Near the village, Mr. Eggenthaler carved a dugout from a cedar log. He found comfort keeping his hands busy, he confided to me, momentarily forgetting the wife who died in childbirth and the baby boy he raised to adulthood only to lose in an accident while trapping on the Mississippi River. Sometimes, he whistled at passing seals and they got curious and swam close to shore.

I loved Indianola in June. Like a firmament of stars, the woods were stippled with the blossoms of dogwood, mock orange, and spirea. Foxglove pushed the dead leaves aside and the delicate new fronds of the sword fern snaked skyward. Wild canaries nibbled the forget-me-nots, and Hanako, quivering with the joy of her new freedom, excitedly stalked a chipmunk inhabiting a hollow log. Out in the bay Virgil stood in a fishing boat bringing good luck to his Indian friends.

When I shut my eyes I heard the lap of water on the beach and sometimes, in the middle of the night, the rush of waves splashing. The ferry booped as it came to dock. When it gnawed against the piling it mimicked the mooing of cows. Caterpillars chewing on alder leaves sounded like rain drops. Most of all I loved the Swainson's thrush, which sang at dawn and dusk with rising spirals of sweet music.

Mom and Aunt Vi moved over for the month of July. They spent their mornings helping Grandpa in the garden or Grandma in the kitchen, canning cherries and making raspberry jam. They enjoyed giggly afternoons lying on the beach. Weekends, Dad and Uncle Tolly came lugging shopping bags of groceries picked up at the Pike Place Market. Aunt Vi called them "our shopping bag daddies."

Now it was wild blackberry time. Frannie and I were off to logged-over areas that had given us good picking last year. It was always a game of hide-and-seek with this tiny native berry. I was spurred on by the sweet smell of the berries mingled with the scent of red cedar. I chased vines that arched over logs and found, like pots at the end of rainbows, clusters of fat, ripe nuggets hiding under the fireweed. Taking home a lard pail of berries was a triumph.

There was a minus-three tide on Sunday, the fifth of July. Grandpa called it a geoduck tide. Frannie and I took our shovels to the beach, crunching over the barnacle-covered rocks to the sandy flat, which stretched all the way to the end of the ferry dock. When we dug for geoducks and horse clams, we looked for the neck of the clam protruding from the sand and dug a trench on three sides. By the time the clam spurted water and started its descent, I was on my knees holding onto its neck. Frannie dug deeper until together we were able to pull the clam out. While we filled our pail and rejoiced over the geoducks we'd caught—the granddaddy of all clams—Hanako did her own digging and got squirted.

Grandma dug butter clams and littlenecks clustered in the rocks nearer the shore, but I preferred the big clams. Once the necks were immersed in boiling water the brown skin peeled off easily and the necks, along with the foot and mantle of the clam when put through a meat grinder, produced a bowl of glistening white meat. Frannie liked to add eggs and onion to make clam burgers. Grandma made chowder with bacon, potatoes, onion, garlic, and condensed milk, topped with a pat of butter. Because butter was getting hard to come by, we had to be satisfied with white margarine made yellow with a pellet of food dye and blended with a fork.

When the tide came in over the hot sand it was perfect for swimming—cold enough to be exhilarating, but not freezing. One day after a swim, I draped my towel over a log and stretched out in the sun. With my eyes closed I could hear the squeak of oars in their locks from across the bay, sea gulls mewing, children laughing, and the thum-thum-thump of someone's hammer. Leaves rustled as a squirrel hurried by. Hanako, asleep, whimpered in a dream.

We were spending our summer in paradise. How come we were so lucky with most of the world in chaos? Why was Frannie so moody?

"All the boys are gone except for a couple of 4-Fs in the village," Frannie complained. "I'm treading water. I'm young and at my best and getting nowhere. Working for women's wages I'll never do anything or be anyone important." Frannie had confessed to me to having had a devastating dream about growing old as a single lady.

"You've got a Cinderella complex," I told her. "You want a prince to appear, fall in love with you at first sight, and sweep you off your feet. You may never get a big wedding or a bungalow with a white picket fence. You may have to settle for an ordinary guy and end up perspiring over the canning kettle like our mothers do and struggling to stretch the budget to buy tennis shoes for your kids. That's life."

Frannie stuck out her tongue and mimicked me. "That's life."

Walking the quarter mile to the ferry each morning was think time. On the hour's ride to town, I read a book or stared into space until Frannie and I joined the commuters at the gangplank. One day I read an article in *Collier's* by Martha Gellhorn, War Correspondent, who was in my opinion the only woman in the world with an exciting job.

"Miss Gellhorn was in Spain, Finland, and China during their bombings," I told Grandpa as he settled down with a cigar on the porch after supper. "The war has changed her. She used to believe in the perfectibility of man and inevitability of progress. Grandpa, the war has changed me too. I want to believe in the destiny of man, but do we get better?"

"Some things get better."

"Who am I? Why am I here? What is the purpose of my existence?"

Grandpa looked peevish as though I'd tossed him a hot biscuit. "Robin, you want everything cut and dried. You'll search all your life and never find answers to those questions. That's life."

Robin's Album

Kiko, Tadashi and I graduated in 1941
and the twins attended University in the fall.
I passed my Civil Service exam and went to work for the
U.S. Army Engineers.

Tadashi says that I am a good Hakujin.

I took a picture of Kiko on a trip to Bainbridge Island.

Grandpa gave me this picture of his old fliwer on the dock at Indianola before the advent of the ferries. The dog's name was Useless.

Mom posed for me on the ferry Illahee.

Hanako loved Indianola—
The root of a huge
Cedar tree is our
favorite place to climb.

Frannie and I love to dig for
geoducks and horse clams.

We took
Hanako for a
rowboat ride.

Hanako and
I watched
the sun set
behind the
Olympics.

13

Sunday mornings I carried my Underwood portable out to the picnic table under Grandpa's apple tree to write letters.

My first was always to Tadashi, and it was as though he were sitting opposite me. Sometimes I answered Kiko's letters, which were slow to come. Out of duty, I wrote to my brother Chris, who was in flight training in Oklahoma. Out of pity, I cranked out letters to David at the CO camp in Oregon. Out of curiosity, I kept in touch with Stony, stationed at APO 948, which Goldie Mae said was Project A in the Aleutians.

I moved back to town from Indianola at the end of August, close to the time when the Japanese were to be moved to Idaho from Camp Harmony, the relocation center on the fairgrounds in Puyallup. Tadashi said they'd be almost a thousand miles from Seattle. Couldn't I come see him while they were only thirty miles away?

The problem was how to get there. Because of gas rationing, many intercity buses were not running on Sunday. It was a surprise when Dad offered to drive me.

"I have an A sticker, which is good for about three gallons of gas a week," Dad explained to me, "provided I can find a station with gas. The car needs a run to keep the battery going."

The following Sunday, I settled into the back seat of Dad's car with Hanako for the ride out through the Kent valley, with Dad conscientiously holding to the legal speed limit of thirty-five miles per hour. On our last drive to Kent the fields and roads were covered with water. Dad had said that someday the U.S. Army Engineers would have to dredge the Green River to prevent the yearly flooding.

As we neared the fairgrounds, Mom said, "I don't see how they managed to squeeze 7,000 people in there. I've heard that they are in animal stalls, under the grandstand, and in tents."

Dad chose to remain in the car with the Sunday paper. Mom wanted to tag along. It was a short walk to the gate. When we got there I was shocked to see the guard tower, soldiers with fixed bayonets on their rifles, and a high metal fence with barbed wire on top. The Nakayama family was imprisoned behind that fence.

When I asked to see Akiko Nakayama the soldier in charge was annoyed. "Which area—A, B, C, or D? We have thousands of people here." Eventually, he checked a notebook and dispatched another soldier to find Kiko.

I felt a drumming on my shoulder. I turned to face a bayonet aimed at my middle. "No pictures allowed here." My camera, which I carried at the end of a crocheted belt, had slipped out from under my jacket.

He followed me to the car, and even after I handed the camera to Dad through the open window, he remained with his bayonet pointed at me.

"What's the matter with you? Stop pointing that thing at me."

The soldier looked surprised, slung the gun over his shoulder, and swaggered back to the gate.

I watched for a long time before Kiko appeared. She looked childlike, with no lipstick, hair straight, wearing an old cardigan I remembered from high school days. She looked nothing like the University freshman who carried herself proudly, with bangs that bounced and a pageboy that undulated with the movement of her head.

"You've lost weight."

Kiko nodded. "I'm down to ninety pounds. I got sick on Vienna sausages the first week we were here. Lots of people got sick. The food was bad at first, but it's better now that we're off the canned stuff. It's hard for Grandmother to adjust to Hakujin food when she has eaten Japanese style all her life."

"Does she still have the canary?"

"No, the canary died the first week we were here; too drafty. Robin, you won't believe it, but we have a shortage of bathrooms and only cold water. Our mattresses are stuffed with hay. We live in a horse stall, and it's impossible to get rid of the smell. We have no privacy in this place. We can hear everything our neighbors say, so we don't talk to each other anymore. A friend of my mother tried to sing a song one evening and the guard told her to shut up."

"Incredible."

"I don't know where I'll be when this war ends. Maybe I won't want to go back to school."

I felt my body sag with disappointment. I had lost my best friend to the university and then to the internment camp.

"Robin, I wonder why that soldier keeps staring at us. Do you suppose he thinks we're plotting to overthrow the government?"

I looked back. One of the soldiers was watching us. He winked at me.

"They tell us we are here for our protection. Why, then, do all the guns point in our direction?"

We watched a Caucasian woman spread a newspaper on the ground so she could sit next to the fence. She knelt on one knee and fell over with legs outstretched, back bowed uncomfortably, while her Japanese friend knelt gracefully and sat on her heels.

I hadn't realized that Tadashi stood nearby until Kiko, seeing Hanako, ran off to find Yuki. I took a deep breath, feeling lightheaded. This was the way it felt to be in love, like teetering on a precipice, knowing that if you fell over, you wouldn't plummet; you'd fly.

Tadashi's eyes clung to mine, changing expressions as thoughts ping-ponged in his head. "Damn this war. Damn this fence. Robin, I just want to be with you."

Before, I hadn't been aware of the clamor around me. Now, it all sorted out. I heard the plane overhead. The soldiers were telling jokes and one of them cackled when he laughed. The little Japanese lady, still sitting on her heels, giggled. In her most authoritative voice, Mom gave instructions to someone on how to make something. Nearby, a group of old men played a game. Those were horseshoes clinking. My nose smarted from dust, a whiff of mold, and the scent of flowers. I wanted to be alone with Tadashi, but there was no place. I was a balloon on a string, and if he grabbed hold, Tadashi could take me anywhere he chose. But he wasn't free.

"I heard Kiko telling you about our hardships here," Tadashi said, leaning as close to me as the fence allowed. "Yuki loves it. She has the run of the place. My parents disapprove, of course. Mother and Grandmother have made new friends and learned some English. But my father has it best of all. He has worked a seven-day week for years. He's having his first vacation, and he enjoys talking to old cronies he hasn't seen in twenty years."

When Kiko returned with Yuki, there was a great hubbub as Mom badgered one of the soldiers to let the dog inside the fence. Finally, a young soldier picked up Hanako, took her through the gate, and handed her to Yuki.

"We've brought you some things," Mom announced, indicating the shopping bags. "Books for you, Kiko, and drawing supplies for Tadashi, and an angel food cake with chocolate frosting."

Tadashi whooped. "Wonderful! We are dying for something sweet."

Mom carefully extracted two bouquets. "These are for your mother and grandmother."

A soldier interrupted her, examining each item. When he opened the box with the cake, he took a knife from his pocket and jabbed it into the middle. The cake, with egg whites energetically whipped by Mom before she added the precious, rationed sugar, slumped from the weight of his knife.

"You've ruined my cake!" Mom cried.

The soldier put the lid back and said, "I'm sorry, ma'am. I'm doing as I was instructed."

Kiko must have noticed Tadashi and me with our heads together. "What's going on?"

Tadashi turned to her with the sweetest smile. "This young lady and I are going to be married. I love her, and I think she loves me."

Kiko gasped. She was too choked up to speak and her eyes brimmed over. She put an arm around her twin and gave him a squeeze.

I think that at that moment the three of us had wonderful things to say to each other, but Mom came alongside me. "Your father was so good about bringing you out here today. I think we shouldn't keep him waiting any longer."

"Don't worry about the cake, Mrs. Mueller. We'll eat every crumb," Tadashi assured Mom as we turned to go.

I was in a daze as Mom rushed me out to the street. There was time only for one last wave.

I lay down on the back seat with Hanako under my chin. Just as I dozed off I heard Mom relate the story of the angel cake. "I'm fit to be tied," she told Dad in a plaintive tone. "That soldier ruined my cake with his dirty old jackknife."

14

Gina returned from North Carolina in October certain that Adrian had shipped out for Africa. As there were no openings in the Dictaphone pool, she took a job upstairs with the Payroll department and spent her lunchtime with me.

Gina had a box full of little red pear tomatoes grown in her parents' garden in Mukilteo. They were delicious with my peanut butter sandwich.

It took me off guard when she asked me to share an apartment. "My aunt is moving to Bellevue. I don't want to commute from there or Mukilteo. We could have a lot of fun together."

"But I don't know how to cook," I stammered.

Gina hooted. "Cooking is fun. I learned lots back East when Adrian and I had a room with kitchen privileges. What do you do when your folks are away?"

"I camp out in my big chair with a book, a bottle of milk, and a box of Ritz crackers."

"Robin, I'll cook, if that makes a difference, and you can set the table and wash dishes."

I was squirming now. "I'd miss my piano. And what would I do about Hanako? My parents would be scandalized if I left home. According to them, nice girls never live by themselves. It isn't safe." I paused to take a breath. I was embarrassed, especially when Gina laughed. "Please, don't laugh, Gina. The real reason is I'm afraid that I will be unable to support myself."

Gina turned serious. "That's what the Depression did to you. You'll get over it."

Two nights later, pounding on the front door awakened me. Dad hurried downstairs, the door slammed, and seconds later, Frannie burst into my room.

"Will you put me up for a few nights? I'm homeless. My father locked me out."

"Whatever for?"

"My date took me to the Trianon tonight and I lost track of the time. He rushed to get me home by one o'clock and got pinched for speeding. That delayed us some, but I wasn't more than a half hour late. My father humiliated me in front of my date."

Frannie dug into my drawer for a nightgown. "He wants to keep me under his thumb. Well, he's lost me now. I'll never go back home. I'll find an apartment. How about your sharing one with me?"

"Gina wants to share an apartment."

"Fantastic." Frannie turned out the light and burrowed under the covers next to Hanako.

I was amazed when Frannie and Gina rented a houseboat on the east side of Lake Union. How had they found a place so easily? People looked for months and city officials warned war workers not to send for their families because of the housing shortage in Seattle.

When Mom learned about the houseboat she bristled like a pillbox with guns sticking out. "Those girls are in a pickle. They'll be surrounded by unsavory characters, outcasts, bootleggers, drunks, communists, and prostitutes. Don't you get any ideas," she warned me.

When I took the bus out Eastlake Avenue and walked down the hill to the lake, I found that the houseboat community reminded me of the old Hoovervilles built on tide flats south of town, only recently torn down. The buildings there had been smaller, made out of wooden crates, ramshackle shanties of cardboard, scrap wood, and corrugated metal sheeting, even rowboats that sheltered one occupant from the rain. Here was a hodgepodge of dwellings on a much grander scale, connected with the land by floating piers, with as many as seven or eight cottages to a row, and some of the piers branched off in different directions. Besides people there were plenty of cats and ducks in residence. One cat was hopping from roof to roof with a kitten in her mouth.

Frannie and Gina occupied a houseboat built on huge cedar logs. On my first visit, I found them painting orange woodwork white. It looked blobby as though every new renter during the past four decades had applied a new coat.

"It'll look swell when we get our furniture," Frannie said, her eyes aglow. "Until then we'll sleep on the floor. We pay $10 a month and we even have an electric stove."

There were two small bedrooms and a combination kitchen-living room. "We could make room for you in the living room," Gina said, hopefully. "We've met all our neighbors on our dock. The girl on the end is a dancer in a burlesque show, and she also belly dances and does hog calling. Her husband is a one-armed drummer."

Frannie dipped her brush in the paint and drained the excess on the rim of the can. "The older people here are migrant workers, loggers, fishermen, and merchant seamen. The young guys are mostly graduate students from the U." Frannie pulled a rug aside to reveal a trap door. "They used this space during Prohibition days to hide their booze. Our friend, Bing, who lives next door, says that because state liquor laws are so restrictive we still have bootleggers around."

"Our landlady has been all over the world," Gina added. "She biked around Europe and stayed at youth hostels. She saw Hitler once, and she says he's short and pasty-faced."

"How are you and Frannie getting along?" I asked Gina one day at lunch.

"Frannie's a riot. She keeps me from getting blue. She makes a ceremony out of taking a bath, sits in her bubbles with candles and incense burning and sings. She sponges up all those tunes on the Hit Parade and the singing commercials and doodles on everything, mostly women with marcelled hair and spiked heels. When she goes out on a date, she takes all the precautions in the advertisements about halitosis and BO."

Frannie and Gina bought a chicken for Thanksgiving. It took hours to bake because of the storm that rocked the houseboats. Bing explained that the oven element in their electric stove connected and disconnected as the wind blew and the houseboats rocked.

It was getting hard for women to come up with holiday fare. Grocery shelves were empty and twenty items were rationed, including meat. Now one had to buy food with red and blue tokens that were like small poker chips. The red point coupons were for meat, butter and fats; the blue for canned and processed foods. Horsemeat and eggs were replacing beef and poultry, and coffee was made of soybeans and cracked wheat. Mom and Aunt Vi stood in line for hours to buy groceries for the holidays.

I was sorry about going to Indianola for Thanksgiving instead of joining Frannie and Gina. It was galling to listen to the trouncing the family gave them. Two young girls, barely twenty, had no business living in an apartment alone, especially a houseboat. No good would come of it, even though one of them was married. They were taking a dwelling from some poor defense worker's family.

Gina planned to go home to Mukilteo for Christmas, so Frannie joined us, and even with her there, the holiday was doomed. Frannie and Uncle Tolly were still not speaking. When Frannie went to bed immediately after the gift exchange, Aunt Vi exploded.

"What's the matter with this family? Can't we come together in harmony on Christmas, for goodness sake?"

An awkward silence followed, which Uncle Fritz was only too willing to fill. "What do you think of the Great White Father now?" he asked Grandfather. "I hate his gaudy guts. But more than him, I hate that wife of his with her overflowing mouth. First Ladies should be gagged the moment their husbands take office."

Grandma, Aunt Vi, and Mom looked hurt as though this latest attack on Eleanor Roosevelt was an attack on them.

Uncle Fritz turned to me. "What are you doing with all that money you earn?"

Before I could think of an answer, Mom said proudly, "She pays me board and the rest she banks. She spends very little on herself."

"You should be finding a good man and settling down."

"First, I'm going to college," I announced.

"Whatever for? To learn to cook?"

"To study journalism."

Uncle Fritz guffawed. "You don't need a college education to write for the women's page—obituaries, marriage notices, and what Mrs. Dokes wore to the party. You should spend your money on things for your hope chest."

"You're wasting your breath, Fritz," Mom said. "These harum-scarum girls have jobs now. They can thumb their noses at us."

I had to admit that Uncle Fritz was right about the newspapers. There were no good jobs for women on the Seattle *Times*. For every Miss Gellhorn, there were probably a million women throughout the nation working at menial jobs for small pay. Maybe it wouldn't always be that way.

I turned twenty in January 1943. In January, people who had been discouraged with the progress of the war felt heartened by news of the German withdrawal from Stalingrad. In February, the Japanese evacuated Guadalcanal, and in March, Allied land-based planes defeated the Japanese in the Battle of the Bismarck Sea.

News from the Minidoka Relocation Center came to me from Tadashi and Kiko. The previous September Tadashi had worked outside the camp to help in Idaho's beet harvest. In October Kiko was hospitalized for ptomaine poisoning along with 160 other evacuees. On January 20th, the mercury dropped to twelve degrees below zero at the camp and Kiko had gone to bed to keep warm. In spite of cold and sickness everyone kept busy. Kiko adopted Yuki's troop of Girl Scouts. There were classes, fund drives, and dances.

In February when the camp chose a Sweetheart of Minidoka, I felt depressed. What was to keep Tadashi from meeting a beautiful Japanese girl at one of the dances? Out of 10,000 people, there had to be hundreds of young women and I imagined that all of them had their eyes on him. It was very reassuring when he started phoning me on Sunday mornings.

He sounded close as though he were calling from a booth downtown. There wasn't any of the static one expected on a long-distance call and I didn't have to shout in a nervous effort to span the miles. My family used long distance only to report a death in the family, so Mom's getting suspicious was to be expected.

I had scurried back to my room when I heard Mom call me from downstairs. "Robin, come here a minute."

I found her and Dad standing by the potbellied stove with dour expressions on their faces. Mom sounded breathless. "You've been cow-eyed for weeks. What's going on? Why is Kiko's brother calling you long distance?"

I wriggled self-consciously. Then, without thinking twice, I blurted, "Tadashi and I are going to get married."

The expressions on my parents' faces did not change. It was as though their heads were full of marbles rolling out and going clunk, clunk, clunk. When my mother finally spoke, she sounded like a robot giving a prepared speech.

"I was glad that you had a friendship with Kiko. It meant that you learned something about another culture. It broadened your vision and made my life more interesting too. But friendship is one thing, intermarriage is another."

My father fidgeted with the stove lid. "Have you any idea what you're letting yourself in for if you marry a Japanese? You'll be regarded by everybody as no better than a tramp."

"Heaven forbid!" Mom exclaimed. "Don't let your Uncle Fritz learn about this. Our friends would be shocked."

"I think Tadashi and I will make this a better world," I told them.

My father's face turned livid. "Hogwash! By producing half-breeds? And what will your children look like? Will they be Buddhists? What makes you think his family will be overjoyed at having you?"

I stood behind the davenport, my fingers tracing the ridges in the upholstery. The dull ache inside my eyeballs began to throb.

My father leaned toward me threateningly. "I can't believe you'd do this to us. I can't even imagine what your kids would look like. It's disgusting. Think, Robin. Just think for once."

Mom gasped. "You wouldn't become a Buddhist, would you?"

Dad brushed Mom aside. "The Buddhists go in for idol worship like the Catholics."

"What idols?"

"Those ugly statues. You had your picture taken with one in Kiko's garden."

"Kwanon isn't ugly. I think she's lovely. She represents the concept of compassion. Buddhists don't worship idols."

"How come you think you know so much?"

"I asked questions. You act as though Buddhism is something bad."

"Well, isn't it?"

"No, Dad, it's a wonderful philosophy of life. The Buddhists I've met are good people."

"Can you honestly say they haven't tried to convert you?"

"No, they wouldn't do that. I've never heard any of them say a bad word about other religions. That's not the way they are."

Mom reminded me of a little engine going up a steep grade, heart pounding and struggling for breath. "Why couldn't you choose David or that nice boy from Arkansas? They are fine young men who could give you a decent life. What in the world do you see in Kiko's brother?"

"Tadashi is the kindest person I know. We understand each other. I enjoy being with him." I wanted to say that I loved him, but I didn't dare. To them, love was frivolous.

"Tadashi has two eyes, a mouth and nose. What makes him so different from us?" Too late I realized I'd cornered Dad.

"You bring him home and I'll kill the bastard."

I stepped back as though he had slapped me. I took a deep breath and said in a calm voice, "Daddy, I'm twenty years old now. I'm not a little girl anymore."

"Then it's time for you to pack your bags and get out."

"No!" my mother cried, and to my amazement she straightened her back and glowered at him. "You're not going to put Robin out. Robin isn't going to marry a Japanese. She's too smart for that."

15

Mom apologized for Dad the next morning at breakfast. "I don't know what gets into these men," she spluttered. "He should have learned from what happened to Tolly. That old goat estranged Frannie for good, apparently, and Violet is miserable."

"They don't want their daughters to have minds of their own."

"Well, now, I wouldn't go so far as to say that. They have to protect their daughters."

"Did Grandpa protect Rose and Pansy? Did Uncle Tolly protect Frannie when he locked her out? How did Dad protect me when he told me to pack my bags and get out? They act like Juliet's father, the proud Capulet who threatened to throw his fourteen year old daughter into the street if she didn't marry the man he had chosen for her."

Mom scanned the ceiling in a show of bewilderment and then changed the subject. "You should quit work before the war winds down and get yourself enrolled at the University." She smiled sweetly. "Your grandfather didn't send any of his four daughters to college, but I'll see that his granddaughter goes with the cookie jar money."

"No, no, Mom. I don't want to get my board money back. That's your money and I want you to have fun with it."

We cleared the table of breakfast dishes, and then as I sat down to finish my coffee she pulled up a chair and grabbed my hands. "Remember when you crawled into bed with me on summer evenings and we listened to the Standard Symphony Hour with the old crystal set? You were such a little girl then. I've seen you change so much since you graduated from high school." She looked down at my hands. "You have beautiful, capable hands."

I squirmed. It wasn't often that Mom got sentimental.

Several days later no mention had been made of Tadashi, as though by ignoring his existence he ceased to be. Did they expect him to disappear from my life so easily? Dad avoided me, responding to my "Hi" with a grunt.

The night I came home to a cold, dark house, Mom was in bed. This would be another scrambled egg night for Dad and me.

While Dad fired up the furnace, I started fires in the kitchen range and the living room stove. Then I went upstairs to see Mom. She was balled up under the covers and didn't show her face until I poked her. Her eyes were puffy.

"Are you worried about Chris?" I asked her.

"Yes, I'm worried about both of you, and I'm worried about myself. I feel so useless. I'm forty-four years old and haven't done anything special with my life. Today the Fuller Brush man came by and he treated me like a dumb cluck. I think he was angry because he had to be nice to this fuddy-duddy in order to make a sale."

"You need an adventure, Mom. You could get a job easily now because of the labor shortage. Boeing will train you. That would take your mind off Chris a bit. Working would be good for Aunt Vi too."

"Ha! You're goofy if you think Tolly would let Violet work. Not on your life. Your father wouldn't allow me, either. Who would stoke the furnace four times a day? Who would let the dog out? With me playing Rosie the Riveter we'd never get food on the table."

"We three could work that out and you would earn your quarters for Social Security."

I was disgusted with her. This talk about college all of a sudden, the tears, the self-pity were all ploys. Mom would do anything to stop my marriage to Tadashi.

I sat down on the edge of the bed and Mom hoisted herself up on her pillow. "I'm sorry, Robin. I'd rather you didn't see me when I'm down in the dumps. I'm ashamed to admit it, but I think I'm jealous of you and your generation. My friends and I didn't have many opportunities. We spent our leisure time crocheting, embroidering, and knitting antimacassars, doilies, and pillowslips, and waited for the right man to come along. It was boring. Of course we had fun too, pulling taffy and having pillow fights at our slumber parties. I had lots of little candles burning brightly in those days, but they've all been snuffed out. Now that you and Chris are grown no one needs me anymore, and the world has no need of me either."

Mom looked so innocent, so vulnerable, so guileless, her eyes clear and luminous. The vision of the world turning its back on Mom was more than I could bear.

"I love you, Mom," and I was surprised to hear myself say that because in our family no one ever said they loved each other. I guess we took it for granted. I reached for her and kissed and hugged her. "This house would be a dungeon without you. Dad and I would be lost souls. We've made a slave out of you. You need something all for yourself. Maybe you should go on a trip. You and Aunt Vi could start a little business. Why don't you learn to drive? You could join a book club or volunteer. There has to be a way for a smart woman to be needed in this world. Oh, Mom, you've got to light those candles again."

Here I was, mothering my own mother, but it worked. Mom got up, put on her robe and slippers and followed me downstairs. Dad had to make another helping of scrambled eggs.

When David Engstrom called me at the office, he was between trains. Would I have dinner with him? He was waiting in the lobby at five, looking handsome in a grey tweed suit.

We walked uptown to Meves' Cafeteria, which was on the second floor of a triangular building between the Bon Marché and Frederick & Nelson. After serving our stint in line we sat down to big bowls of clam chowder with buns.

"I'm on my way to Rapid City, South Dakota to be reassigned," he told me. "Wyeth Station is like the end of the world. It's an old CCC camp in the Columbia Gorge where the river cuts through the Cascade Range. It wasn't the loneliness that got me. The COs there are Mennonites and Brethren and very religious."

"Where will you go now?"

"I want to be with the Quakers. They're an intellectual bunch and most of them work in mental hospitals. I need to get transferred to a camp near a university so I can get credits in my spare time. I've volunteered for a study on atypical pneumonia that will give me some option as to where I go."

"What's atypical pneumonia?"

"I don't know, but a lot of soldiers get it, and the Army wants to know why."

"David, don't let them inoculate you with a germ. You could get sick for the rest of your life. What good would a college education do you then?"

He smiled briefly as though he were pleased that someone cared, but his face was flushed. "Conscientious objectors don't get paid, Robin. The money I earned for college goes for my keep and travel. It cost me $35 a month at Wyeth Station. I hope my money lasts because I don't want to rely on the Quakers for my support. I'm in a vacuum until this war is over. Then I'll have to earn money to go to school. It'll be a long time before I can..." and he stopped.

I knew exactly what he wanted to say. I also knew that if I flirted a little, he would beg me to wait for him.

As we walked down First Avenue past the penny arcades and pawn-shops, he repeatedly smashed his left palm with his right fist. "In this popular war called the people's war, about one out of every 1,000 men ask to be classified 1-O, or exempt from military service because of religious convictions against war. Why don't our leaders have a duel and get it over with? Why should it always be the young men to be slaughtered?"

After he put me on the Yesler bus, I saw him head in the direction of King Street Station.

❀

I worried about David for a couple of days until I got a raging toothache and had to urge my dentist to squeeze me in between patients. After checking the tooth, Doc Challis covered my mouth with a rubber dam, punched a hole for the tooth and tied the four corners around my head. A suction device removed saliva so that I didn't have to spit into the receptacle that stood to the left of the dental chair.

"Now you look like a clam swirled in seaweed," he said, laughing. "Are your folks putting in a victory garden this year? Tell them it's getting hard to find seeds. I lug home pails of kelp and seaweed for fertilizer. The best stuff is that dirty black muck off the beach. It stinks, but my kale grows big on it." The hair on Doc Challis' head stood stiffly like a forest of bristles.

It was hard to concentrate on what he said while my mind churned with thoughts. Someday David would be a college professor and spend his summers on Indian reservations or archeological digs in Mexico and South America. Whatever David's wife's interests were, they'd take a back seat.

Doc Challis interrupted my thoughts. "Do you know how the silent letter originated in the Russian language? Long ago it was thought that the superiority of male over female could be demonstrated with flourishes in the written language, but when it got to be too much work to embellish masculine nouns, they limited the art work to the ends of words."

I stared at the light above the dental chair. Trouble was, I wanted to make everybody happy, especially my parents, but that was impossible. No matter whom I married, there'd be a fuss. I could hear Mom say, "I'll put up a squawk if you marry that Conshie."

"We bathe too much," Doc Challis said as he probed my tooth. "If we remained dirty like the savages, we'd have better teeth. We wash away the Vitamin D."

Suddenly, in a flash of insight I realized that for years Mom had prepared me for a loveless marriage. To her, passion was indecent.

"I keep a cat at my beach shack," Doc Challis said while pausing briefly to look out the window. "Last weekend I caught five bullheads and five kelp cod. I cleaned all ten fish and dumped them in a pan. When they were done I tasted one of the bullheads and it was good, so I gave the cod to the cat and ate the bullheads myself. The cat didn't know the difference."

Someday Tadashi and I would stroll across campus on our way to classes and maybe we'd live in an apartment overlooking University Way. I felt a big tear roll down my cheek and under the rubber dam.

"You aren't hearing a word I'm saying. I'll bet you're in love and your sweetie is a long way from here."

"Uh-huh," is all I managed to say.

"Well, I'm sorry this war is keeping you two apart. It's too bad man has to solve his problems with wars. Man needs an enemy, an evil to fight. You can sell him anything except brotherly love."

16

On March 17th Goldie Mae came to work with a newspaper under her arm.

"Robin, did you see last night's paper?" She spread the Seattle *Times* on her desk. The headline read: TRICKERY SAVED ALASKA FROM INVASION BY THE JAPS. No, I hadn't seen the paper.

"That's a helluva note! Don't you ever read the paper? Or do you spend all your spare time contemplating your navel? You were the one who took the call from Colonel Talley last June when he tried to tell Colonel Goertz what had happened up there, and the censor broke in. According to the Alaska Defense Command, a Japanese invasion force attacked Dutch Harbor that day and our planes from Project A scared them away."

"No kidding!" I exclaimed, and I wondered if Stony or Tyler were involved in that skirmish.

"Hell's bells, it took nine months to hit the papers. Isn't that a kick in the pants? We helped build that airfield typing those requisitions on New Year's Eve and New Year's Day. The Japanese thought Project A was a salmon packing company. I can tell you now that Project A is Umnak in the Aleutians. Without Umnak, Dutch harbor didn't have one protecting airfield within 800 miles."

So, we were a part of the war effort after all. My job had become routine. Now that lightweight books called paperbacks had invaded the market, I carried a couple in my purse for reading on the bus and at work whenever there was a lull, and there were plenty of those.

When Goldie Mae announced that she and her husband were moving back to San Antonio, I was alarmed. How could I survive without her and Gina? I didn't feel close to any of the other members of the pool.

On Goldie Mae's last day, after the calls were logged and the cylinders filed away, we took her to dinner at the Rathskeller, a pub adjacent to the Maison Blanc. "I won't forget you gals," she assured us. "I'll always remember those first few weeks of the war when we expected the worst. Remember the policeman who sat next to us all day, guarding the secret files?" She directed her attention to Garnie, a comparative newcomer to the pool. "They moved us to lobby six on the first floor after the Engineers began to expand all over town. It was a big hole in the wall with no windows, only a skylight that they painted black on our first day there. I was madder'n a wet hen. We had nothing but artificial light for days on end. We got away from the drafty basement, but lobby six was an oven in summer and that drove me bughouse. After much bellyaching, we got to move to where the Japanese bank had been. Windows at last."

I loved Goldie Mae, a brash, free spirit with a raucous laugh. I wanted to be just like her. Before the taxi whisked her away she gave me a big hug.

The next morning Clara sat at Goldie Mae's desk and I knew she would be our new supervisor. She had the power to make my life miserable and she started right away by demanding that I copy one page over because of a small error.

After the others filed out for lunch, I returned the government manifold to my desk drawer and filled a paper bag with stationery, Kleenex, mug, spoon, knife, two books and a small dictionary. I headed for the waterfront near Colman Dock and Ye Olde Curiosity Shop where I fed my lunch to the sea gulls. I was scared. What if I couldn't find another job?

I decided to see the Personnel Director immediately. I expected him to be austere, but Mr. Ulvestad turned out to be warm and friendly. "Miss Mueller, your former supervisor wanted you to replace her. It would be impossible for me to put a twenty-year-old girl in charge of eight women, all older than she. Your supervisor was ill-advised. Now that more projects are out of the initiation stage so that there's little construction going on up north, there will be layoffs. It's time for an intelligent young person like yourself to move on."

He closed my file and drummed on it with his fountain pen.

"We have an agency opening up called the Twelfth Regional War Labor Board. The chairman is a political science professor from Reed College. We need a secretary for the Labor members on the Board. I'd like to offer you that job."

"What does this agency do?" I asked, stalling for time.

"The Public members help the Labor and Industry members come to agreement on labor issues. You'll meet interesting people on this job. I'll send your papers over this afternoon."

I needn't have felt uncomfortable about the new job. I met Marcelyn, the chairman's secretary, on the elevator and she introduced me to Kathy, recording secretary of the Board, and Jane, the secretary to the Industry members.

Marcelyn was short and plump with thick glasses and she wore a cashmere sweater, a pleated skirt, and casual shoes as though she were still on campus. "Dr. Noble was my professor at Reed College," she told me. "He is helping me get my doctorate."

"Don't take off your shoes," Jane advised me. "Marcy will make them disappear and you'll have to go around in your stockings."

"We play a little," Kathy said, "but we work hard too. Last week I covered a board meeting until two in the morning."

I was exploring my desk when Dr. Noble greeted me. "Welcome aboard," he said as he shook my hand.

By ten o'clock the office had turned into a beehive with professors, a handsome priest, Labor leaders and Industry members swarming all over the place, even reporters and news photographers. When the Board went into session, Marcelyn and Kathy disappeared and Jane and I were left to answer telephones.

One afternoon while Dr. Noble was away, Jane brought back from the Swiss Pastry Shop an assortment of little cakes, all different and beautifully decorated. "Where do they get the sugar?" I asked.

"On the black market, probably," Kathy guessed.

"No, they get a good allowance because without it their business would fail," Marcelyn explained.

"There are no sweets in the dime stores now, only nuts," Jane complained. "You can't get a decent meal downtown anymore. They don't butter the sandwiches and the soda I had yesterday was sour. A friend sent me maple sugar candy and it tasted good."

"Everybody says rationing is here to stay."

When I arrived home the odor of pork backs and necks simmering in sauerkraut on the wood range permeated the house. As I sat down at the kitchen table I announced, "I love my new job."

Mom made happy noises, but Dad looked at me thoughtfully. "Don't work too hard. While you slave, the others will play politics, loaf and gossip."

I was amazed to hear this from my hard-working father. He could be right. I didn't want to end up in some poorly lit back room cutting stencils all day, stapling mimeographed sheets and doing copy work. If I made myself useful by keeping my eyes and ears open, by reading the directives, and learning how to give out the information everybody needed, I might become a valuable addition to the War Labor Board.

Eventually, all the Labor members stopped by to say hello. Mr. Hood liked to sit on my desk and talk. One day he told me about his going to World War I with an Australian outfit. "I started over a hill with two of my buddies and the first one got hit by artillery fire. The second man and I stood there picking pieces of his body off of us. The second guy went stark raving mad on the spot. From what I've heard, he has spent his life in an institution in Canada."

Nick Katudy was the Labor member I liked the most. He was in his sixties with a full head of black hair tinged with white around his face, a triangular groove between his chin and nose that framed his mouth, and inquisitive eyes peering out from his scraggly brows.

"I hear you're a pacifist," he said one day.

"I have leanings in that direction. That's all."

"Eventually you'll learn that little is gained in this world without struggle. For almost two decades Mussolini has been the absolute master of thirty million people. A state that squashes the right to strike is a slave state. If you lived in Italy you'd be part of the underground, waiting for a chance to overthrow the government."

"Me? I'm not a fighter."

"I don't believe it. Anyone with strong convictions and a sense of justice is bound to be a fighter. You haven't found the cause of your heart yet. When you do, you'll spend your life with it."

A week later, Mr. Katudy told me to throw my sandwich in the wastebasket. "I'm taking you to lunch."

As we ate spaghetti and garlic bread at the Italian Village, he told me the story of his life. "My mother died when I was eight years old. The embalmers came into the family living room and worked on her body right in front of me. I lived with an aunt until she died and at twelve I had to pick up coal along the railroad tracks to sell for food. I was fourteen when I shipped out." Mr. Katudy pushed his plate away.

"I became a logger, got involved with the unions, and joined the Wobblies. I'll bet you don't know what Wobblies are?"

"Yes, I do. My grandfather was a Wobbly."

"Well, good. We got the Wobblies moniker because the Chinese couldn't pronounce the three R's in our name. At that time, conditions in the woods were bad, real bad. People got killed or maimed for life and there was no compensation. I never could understand why people hated us so much. We were militant and they were afraid of us. They said we were un-American and they tried to run us off. We wanted decent working conditions, that's all.

"I was in Centralia at the time of the massacre in 1919. When we got into a fracas with the American Legion they wanted to demolish our office. Four of the American Legion guys were killed and one of ours got strung up and emasculated on a bridge leading into town. That kid was only thirty-two years old. And he was a vet too.

"The next day, people came out of the woods from everywhere. They didn't dare raise their voices against the American Legion, but they stood in silent protest in the most moving demonstration I've ever seen."

Life was good. I enjoyed my job, and I put money in the bank every payday for my future college expenses. And Tadashi called me on Sundays around ten o'clock in the morning.

If I caught the call, the operator said, "I have a long distance call for Robin Mueller." When Mom caught it, she said, "You've got a long distance call. What a waste of money. Such foolishness." She never said, "You've got a call from Tadashi." As far as my parents were concerned, Tadashi didn't have a name.

There were four doors leading into our hall, always closed to conserve heat. A large drapery hung over the opening to the upstairs. We had to stand in order to reach the mouthpiece and to accommodate the receiver, which was on a short cord.

My call didn't come through until late afternoon. "I'm in Chicago, Robin," I heard him say. "I enlisted in the Army and I'm on my way to Hattiesburg, Mississippi."

I can't remember what I said because I was so shocked. Tadashi pinned me down with words as effectively as if he'd pushed my shoulders against a wall.

"Robin, please don't chastise me. I did what I had to do. My mother cried, my father swore in Japanese, Akiko lectured me, and Yoshio walked out on me. I know you'll think I'm trying to prove my loyalty. It's more than that. I can't sit around camp doing nothing while other guys are risking their lives. This is my country too."

Kiko's letter came the next day. "The Army came to Minidoka seeking recruits. They circulated questionnaires. This camp has been in turmoil ever since. The first question is: *Are you willing to serve in the armed forces of the United States on combat duty, wherever ordered?*

"How would you like it if you'd tried to enlist and they called you an enemy alien? The second question is even more disturbing: *Will you swear unqualified allegiance to the United States of America and faithfully defend the United States from any and all attacks by foreign or domestic forces, and forswear any form of allegiance or obedience to the Japanese Emperor, or any other foreign government, power, or organization?*

"Robin, if they say 'Yes,' it's like admitting to having held allegiance to the Emperor. That's unfair to the Nisei who are citizens. And it's unfair to the Issei too who were prohibited by law from becoming citizens. And if they say 'Yes,' they have no country to fall back on. If they say 'No,' the government might ship them back to Japan after the war is over. The Nisei who answered 'No' to both questions are called 'No-No Boys' and will be sent to Tulelake, California. Yoshio is one of them. Another friend of Tad's tried to make a test case and they sent him to prison on McNeil Island. Tad answered 'Yes' to both questions and has passed his physical."

I ran upstairs, dove into my big chair and closed my eyes. I could see Kiko's face, eyes flashing, infuriated by the questionnaire that had split her family and caused bad feelings throughout the camp, indignant because the men who volunteered would be in an all-Nisei combat unit instead of dispersed throughout the Army as they wanted to be. It seemed an insult to me to segregate the Japanese recruits, especially when their families were confined to concentration camps.

The next time Tadashi called he told me that he was subject to twenty-six weeks of basic training. "Then I get to come home on furlough, probably in October. How about meeting me in Spokane and we'll get married?"

My heart galloped in circles inside my chest. "Okay," and I tried not to sound excited in case Mom was listening in.

17

I was astonished when Mom announced that Frannie and I would have to spend our summer in town. How come? We had always vacationed at Indianola with Grandpa and Grandma.

"Now that you and Frances are working girls, Grandma should not have to prepare dinners for you every night. She'll get more sleep when she doesn't have to worry about your catching the ferry in the morning. You and Frances can visit in July when Violet and I are there."

I knew that Frannie would gladly stay in town. She loved living in the houseboat with Gina and she had a slug of new boyfriends. With Playland open she'd ride The Dipper every Saturday night.

But I felt abandoned. I loved our little village of Indianola. As spring merged into summer I missed the nettle soup Grandma made with nettles that were young and tender, and dandelion greens sautéed in butter and vinegar. Most of all I missed the sweet sounds of the Swainson's thrush in the early morning and at dusk. Wild blackberry season of early July passed without our yearly visits to secret patches.

When Mom and Aunt Vi moved to Indianola for two weeks to help Grandma with housework and canning, and Grandpa with weeding and gardening, Frannie and I decided to promote a slumber party. Frannie invited Gina and Delaine, and my guests were Marcelyn and Nellie. We were a giggly bunch on the ferry after release from our Saturday jobs. We stopped at the house to introduce our friends before heading down the trail to the beach with sleeping bags and food.

The tide was at its highest. We could hear voices from far away and our laughter probably carried to Suquamish and Bainbridge Island. Because no one can walk the beach during high tide when trees and shrubs hang over the water we had our own private room surrounded by greenery. We sat on the sun-bleached logs, kicked off our shoes, and dipped our toes in the water.

I looked at Frannie and she looked at me. Words were unnecessary. We unzipped our skirts, threw our blouses and slips aside, and dove into the water in our underwear. Delaine, Frannie's friend from grade school days, followed. The others stood gaping at us.

"You're not getting us in that cold water," they shouted.

"It's not so bad," Frannie said without convincing anyone. "The tide has been inching its way over the hot sand all afternoon. We hit little warm currents here and there."

After our dip we dressed and helped the others start a fire and spread the food on the huge cross section of cedar log that was always used as a picnic table. We were hungry.

"Robin is the only one of us who doesn't have to worry about blue and red ration points and save tin foil and grease for the war effort. You have it easy living at home," Gina said.

Delaine prepared a branch to spear a hot dog for roasting in the fire. "I don't begrudge the armed forces the good food they get, but I wish some GI would share a steak with me. I'm starved for a steak. All I get these days is monkey liver."

"What's monkey liver?" we all wanted to know.

"That's our family's name for chipped beef. I keep a supply in my closet. I get it packed in little jelly glasses and after soaking it a bit to get out the salt, I stir it into gravy or white sauce and spoon it over potatoes."

Frannie broke the cellophane on a package of hot dog buns. "My mother and Aunt Daisy talk a lot about one-egg cakes. What's so special about one-egg cakes?"

122

"That's a carry-over from the Depression when eggs were hard to get," Marcelyn explained in her most authoritative manner. "You were lucky to get dessert."

"We can be thankful the Depression is over," I said as I settled my back against a log with Hanako curled up in my lap. "I hated to see men come to our back door begging for food."

"Speaking of hunger, I was the youngest of six kids and we rarely had enough to eat when our father took off for the first war." I could tell by their alert expressions that we were all mesmerized by Nellie's thick English accent. "Every Saturday night, our mum went around the circle with the same spoon and fed each of us bread softened with warm milk and sprinkled with sugar. She called it 'turkey pie,' and we loved it When my brothers were hungry they said it hurt to scratch their heads with a comb. Poor bairns."

"And you remember World War I?" We were amazed. Nellie looked so young. How much older was she than the rest of us who were born after the Armistice?

"I remember the Germans bombing our town from zeppelins. I saw my mum searching through the rubble for her marriage papers. Now she's experiencing all that again. After the Nazis have bombed our cities, they dump what's left on our town. I worry about my parents and my brothers in service. Every time they write to me, a neighbor or friend has been killed."

"How did you happen to come to Seattle?"

"When I was eighteen my mum opened the door and said I was free to go out into the world in search of adventure. I took a boat to the continent where I spent three months bicycling from one youth hostel to another. It cost me one dollar a day, twenty-five cents for overnights and the rest for food."

"She saw Hitler," I interposed.

"Yes. We were in Bad Gödesburg then. People heiled him enthusiastically, but he seemed bored. I went to Australia when the second war started and worked as a nanny. Later, I was a tour guide in Montreal.

Here, I've been 'Bundles for Britain' girl on KJR radio. I'm going to stay in Seattle. I've bought two houseboats, the one Gina and Frannie live in, and my own on another dock. I want to buy scruffy little houses and fix them up."

Delaine leaned toward Gina. "I'm glad you brought a bottle of buttermilk. I like to sieve out the little pieces of butter with my teeth and smash them with my tongue."

"Can you believe it—during that hot spell last week they ran out of Coca Cola and Lime Rickey? Imagine, no pop in Seattle on the hottest day this summer."

And no film for my camera, I thought, remembering how I used to get pictures around the campfire with time exposures and manganese flares.

Frannie pulled up her skirt to show off her leg make-up. "Doesn't it look like I'm wearing stockings?"

"What are you going to do next winter—freeze?"

Frannie shrugged. "I don't know. I took my silk stockings to the hosiery-mending department at Kress' where a lady stretched them over the top of a glass and caught up the runs. She charged fifteen cents for a long run, more for snags. Finally she told me my stockings were beyond repair."

"I'll bet that's the last you'll see of silk stockings," Marcelyn said. "After the war is over silk worms and fast trains to New York will be passé. In the meantime, you'll have to go to rayons."

Frannie made a face. "I hate those baggy things. They're shiny and ugly, and if you bend your knee the bulge stays until you wash it out. Lisle stockings twist around your ankles and make you look like an old lady."

"You're stuck with them for the duration. There'll be no nylons as long as they make parachutes."

"I wish they'd get rid of garters and seams. I hate keeping seams straight and I loathe sitting on garters."

Delaine announced that she planned to join the Women's Army Corps. A friend in the WAC went on a photo mission in a B-17 and the pilot let her fly the plane. We laughed and teased her. "You aren't patriotic. You just want excitement."

Gina was the only married woman among us. She looked glum most of the time, but now and then she cranked up a smile. "Adrian is somewhere in Africa or Sicily. When I don't get any letters, I'm depressed. Once I received ten letters in one day. His letters are getting farther and farther apart and are as much as a month old when I get them. They are shorter and more serious. I can tell he's changed. I'm eager to get a letter dated after the victory in Tunisia."

"He should feel good about that."

Marcelyn ate the last of the potato salad on her plate. "Everyone wants to know what the War Labor Board does. It settles disputes between labor and industry and prevents strikes. This afternoon Dr. Noble took me out to Mitzel's, a de-denting plant on the Duwamish River. I watched them mend, clean, paint and de-dent oil drums. It takes them twelve minutes per drum. If you know anyone who gets less than fifty cents an hour, tell them to apply to the WLB and they'll get a raise automatically."

We all screamed our appreciation when Aunt Vi appeared carrying a wild blackberry pie. Whose sugar went into that, we wanted to know. Aunt Vi stayed with us until we devoured the pie and Frannie had scooped out the juice from the tin. "I've kissed the cook," she said as she licked the spoon.

"How's Kiko?" Gina asked.

"She's working for Administration at Minidoka for $10 a month and she manages a Girl Scout troop. The internees have put in a huge garden, organized a band, and they have dances. They had an arts and crafts exhibit at the Twin Falls Library and they're planning a big Bon Odori festival next month."

Nellie looked pleased. "Sounds like they're getting along okay."

"Kiko wrote to me about an Issei who was stunned to learn that the FBI knew the day he arrived in the United States, the ship he came on, the port he chose when he jumped ship, and the person who had befriended him. That was thirty-three years ago." I was disappointed. No one seemed to think that was unusual.

"Kiko says the British Columbia government treated their Japanese worse than our government did. They confiscated their property, sold it without permission, often at low prices, and charged them commissions for selling it."

The girls were staring into the fire. No one looked up. Did I have to tell them that Tadashi and I were getting married in October to get a rise out of them?

In respect for the rules of warfare we put out the fire when the sun dropped behind the Olympic Mountains. We sang *"A-tisket, a-tasket, a green and yellow basket"* and *Blue Moon*. Nellie taught us the words to the *Sixpence Song* and we joined Frannie in a chorus of *When Love is Kind*.

When the tide had receded below the barnacled rocks, Frannie tried to arouse interest in swimming, but she had no takers, not even those who wanted to see the phosphorescent trails the fish made at night.

When we crawled into our sleeping bags Hanako wiggled in next to me. "You sweetheart," I whispered in her ear, "how can I possibly give you back to Yuki?"

The ground was hard, but we were all asleep the next morning when Grandpa came down to invite us up to the house for breakfast.

In August, Nellie talked me into going on a bicycle trip. The proprietor of Broadway Cycle exchanged Chris' bike for a girl's Raleigh Gazelle.

"That bike came over from England in the first shipment of lightweights to Seattle. The kids will be jealous of you because they have those heavy balloon-tired jobs. You have to go to Canada or Europe to find people who appreciate biking," he said.

I bought saddlebags to hang over the rear tire and a kickstand. I felt exuberant as I wheeled the bike out of the shop.

"You should buy more things for yourself," Nellie advised. "If you leave your money in a bank account, it's like putting all your eggs in one basket. I'm going to buy a scruffy little house, fix it up and rent it, and if there's inflation after the war, my house will rise in value."

Nellie and I biked to Colman Dock and took an old ferry called the *Iroquois*, which left at midnight and was due to arrive in Victoria, British Columbia at eight in the morning. There were at least thirty other cyclists aboard, all friends of Nellie's. Most of the boys were 4-F, she said, or were waiting to be called into service. Everyone unrolled sleeping bags in the area next to the smoke stacks on the top deck.

Canadian bikers were waiting for us as we came out of Customs in Victoria. There were lots of hugs among old friends. I counted sixty-seven bicycles as we moved past the Parliament Building. An old man with a beard bicycled by without glancing in our direction.

"Someday we should bike the Malahat," Nellie suggested as we meandered along Marine Drive. "British Columbia has a loop of hostels and as long as there is gas rationing, the roads belong to us."

Late afternoon as we returned to the harbor, there were so many American and Canadian soldiers and sailors promenading it was like an anthill that has been prodded with a stick.

As summer drew to a close, I spent evenings helping Dad carry eight cords of wood and two loads of planer ends from the backyard into the basement—wood destined for the kitchen range and the potbellied stove in the living room.

Dad worked fast, but whenever he heard a plane, he paused to look skyward. "That's a B-17," he'd say excitedly. "Boeing is turning those babies out like hot cakes."

One of my first memories was of Dad's excitement over seeing the *Spirit of St. Louis* fly overhead when Lindbergh was in town.

Before the month ended, Dr. Noble called me into his office and asked me if I'd be interested in becoming his secretary. "Marcelyn doesn't like clerical work," he explained. "She's going to be my administrative assistant."

When I arrived home, I skipped up the front steps anticipating the looks on my parents' faces when I announced that I was now Secretary to the Chairman of the Twelfth Regional War Labor Board.

As I reached for the door, Mom opened it. She had been crying. "Oh, Robin...Hanako died."

I bolted into the house. "Where is she? Where is she?" On a card table in the dining room was a box. Hanako was wrapped in a sheet inside the box. When I saw Hanako's lifeless body, I sat down on the floor and sobbed.

Mom hovered over me. Finally, she got down on one knee. "She died in her sleep, Robin. The dog had two good summers with us. Dogs and people die when they get old."

"How can I ever tell Yuki?"

"That's Kiko's job, not yours. Now stop it. Stop being silly. After all, she was only a dog."

18

Early in September of 1943, the Allies invaded Italy. Adrian was wounded in the landing on Sicily. Gina said he would be in a hospital in West Virginia for three to six months and then they would go to Arkansas to visit his relatives before returning to Seattle. As she packed for her trip East, she advised me to move in with Frannie. But I had other plans.

I wanted my vacation to coincide with Tadashi's furlough. When I told Mom about visiting the Nakayamas, alarm skipped across her face. Because there had been so little communication between us since the blowup six months ago, she said nothing and I made an easy getaway with my suitcase and Mrs. Nakayama's sewing machine.

Tadashi arranged for me to hitch a ride with the Reverend and his wife who made monthly trips to Minidoka to take items that the internees were unable to obtain through the Sears and Roebuck catalogue. They always spent a night in Spokane, going and coming, and two nights at Minidoka before returning home.

By way of Spokane the trip totaled about 950 miles, a long jaunt at thirty-five miles an hour in an old jalopy that made a lot of noise. We had three flat tires on the way to Spokane. I watched the Reverend pump up the inner tubes and immerse them in a pail of water in order to detect leaks before adding the rubber patches.

As the old car labored to the summit of Snoqualmie Pass and across the eastern Washington plateau, I sat in the back seat with the Reverend's purchases and ruminated over what my parents would consider a betrayal of their trust. They would never forgive me for sneaking off to get married. Why did they hate Tadashi so much? Why? Didn't they want me to be happy? Didn't they? No, they were more concerned about themselves than they were about me. For them, having a Japanese son-in-law was nothing to brag about. I'd have to marry the mayor's son to make them happy.

Out of Spokane, I thought only of Tadashi. There was snow in spots. I shivered in my summer coat, the red one with the black velvet collar. If Tadashi came north in suntans, he'd be shivering too.

He had written me that a soldier could obtain a marriage license and be married the same day. He suggested we ask the Reverend to marry us. He was afraid a justice of the peace in the town near Minidoka might refuse. After all, inter-racial marriage was against the law in California. Maybe it was in Idaho too.

Tadashi's letters bulged with sketches of Camp Harmony in Puyallup, Washington and the camps in Minidoka, Idaho, and Shelby, Mississippi. He pulled beauty from grim scenes, and the internees and soldiers he sketched came to life with a few strokes. He had decided to major in both art and poly sci. "He wants to be a political cartoonist and make fun of the big shots," Kiko wrote. At the time Tadashi encouraged me to make photography my career, he said, "It's the creative process that sets you free and puts you in touch with something bigger than yourself. When I draw, I'm happy."

It was dark when we arrived at camp. After signing in at the guardhouse, the Reverend's wife led me to the building where we were to spend the night. I was disappointed that Tadashi was nowhere to be seen. I'd expected him to be waiting for me at the gate.

Instead, it was morning before I heard the urgent knock on my door. Kiko, looking high school-girlish in a short bob and a white blouse and jumper, grabbed me in a hug and we lost our balance and nearly landed on the floor.

"Robin, I have bad news for you. Tad arrived on Friday and got a telegram the next morning summoning him back to his base. He left immediately."

I sank into a chair. "What does this mean? Is he going overseas?"

"I don't know. One thing's for sure. You two won't be getting married for awhile." Kiko handed me a long box and a tiny one.

There was a scroll in the big box, drawings of chipmunks and birds. "I'm going to frame this," I decided. In the little box was a ring with a tiny green frog on a lily pad. I loved it. "This is going to be my engagement ring."

Eventually, we got caught up with all the happenings of our lives during the year we'd been apart.

When we stepped outside I was amazed to see the rows on rows of tar-papered barracks. "So big!" I exclaimed.

"Ten thousand people," Kiko reminded me.

This was a small town plunked down on a volcanic plain, covered with sagebrush the color of green mold.

"All single construction with no insulation," Kiko said. "When the temperature dropped to twelve below last winter, we went to bed to stay warm."

We dodged mud puddles on our way to the Nakayamas' unit. I knew Grandmother had died. Mrs. Nakayama actually said hello to me in English. Yuki and I cried, remembering Hanako. Mr. Nakayama motioned me into the room that was their home.

In the middle was a potbellied stove with a bucket of coal alongside. There were four Army cots, two at each end of the room. Had Tadashi slept here too? There was no place to wash one's hands, no bathroom. What did they do when there was snow on the ground? How did they get to the open-pit toilets in the middle of the night? How did women manage to care for small children and the elderly with no running water?

They had improvised, apparently. A chamber pot, a pitcher, a washbowl were in evidence; also glasses and cups.

From under his cot Mr. Nakayama pulled out a little three-drawer chest.

"That's a tansu," Kiko explained. "Father made that and the butsudan on the wall, and all our furniture out of scrap lumber." She pointed to the table and benches.

I pulled out the drawers of the tansu and admired the craftsmanship.

"Everybody makes things. Come, I show you." Mr. Nakayama grabbed my arm and took me next door to see Mr. Ito's canes. Mr. Ito's collection was mounted on the wall of the room. Some were bright yellow with brown streaks; others were twisted into strange shapes with burls for handles.

"Where did you get the wood?" I asked.

"He get permission to go on prairie. Lots of bushes called bitterbrush and greasewood out there. He make canes out of that stuff."

Mr. Ito laughed happily. "Don't you go out there without boots. Lots of rattlesnakes and scorpions."

Mr. Nakayama took me to see the rock garden built by Mr. Kojita and the collection of stones Mr. Takamura painted to look like people. Someone else he knew made musical instruments, and he had heard about an Issei who trained birds.

On the way back, he showed me the 270 acres the internees had transformed into farmland after digging a seven-mile-long irrigation ditch. The remaining pumpkins and squash were vestiges of a bumper crop.

"Next year we plant more. Lots more," he said.

When it was time for church, we walked to the recreation hall, which served as Buddhist Temple on Sunday mornings and was also used for classes and movies. I was familiar with the Buddhist chanting and I liked the fragrance of burning incense, which symbolically purifies the mind and body.

After the long sermon in Japanese, the younger sensei told the story of a Buddhist disciple who, while being stalked by a tiger, found refuge in an abandoned well only to discover that he must hang onto branches of a thorn bush growing from the bottom to keep from falling to where cobras lay in wait. Halfway down the well, a white mouse and a black mouse gnawed at the trunk of the thorn bush. He had disturbed a hive of bees, which covered him with stings, but by leaning his head back he could catch drops of honey with his mouth. When help arrived he didn't want to leave until the honey supply was exhausted.

Kiko explained. "This legend illustrates the unending predicament of humanity. No one escapes suffering in this life. Our suffering is prolonged by our attachment to the honey. Buddhism is the search for enlightenment as a way out of suffering."

Later we stood in line for lunch at the mess hall. The mashed potatoes, sausages, canned green beans, and rolls were not favorite foods of the Japanese.

"What, no rice, no bok choy, no Napa cabbage?"

Kiko looked amused. "Yes, we get rice, but you know me. I could eat it three times a day. We haven't seen soy sauce in a long time. At least we have good cooks here, and the food is better than it was at Puyallup where we never got enough."

After we finished our lunch we huddled at the end of one of the long tables. "We have thirty-five mess halls for everybody at Minidoka and four deep wells to provide water. The contractor dug only one ditch for water and sewage, so our well water has to be chlorinated. It's a good thing we raised a lot of our own food this summer because when the trucks come in, they often carry only half the stuff listed on the bills of lading."

"How come?"

"Our food is stolen along the way. I think they planned this camp from 1930 census data, because the units are suitable for bachelors, not families. Those 1930s bachelors got married and produced kids."

I bent closer. "I want to know how you are, Kiko. What's going on in your life?"

"Not much. I enjoy working at the Administration Building. I can't get interested in the craft classes or the clubs. I read everything I can get my hands on."

"You get bored?"

"I feel like I'm endlessly waiting. They've got a big map of the world in the building where I work with flags marking all the places battles are being fought. Those flags never seem to move."

Aunt Kazzie and Uncle Daisho were the only people I recognized until Yoshio poked his head in the door.

"He's crazy," he said to me.

"Who? Tadashi?"

"Anybody who fights for a country that keeps his parents behind barbed wire. How can he ignore the conditions here? They've got searchlights going at night. A sleepwalker could end up shot in the back. They killed one old guy."

Because Yoshio was a "No-No Boy" and Tadashi had answered "Yes-Yes" on the government questionnaire, a beautiful friendship had ended. What a pity, I thought; remembering the fun these two had shared. As children Tadashi and Yoshio swam in the old Japanese baths in the basement of the Panama Hotel across the street from the Golden Pheasant. Once Tadashi had said with a grin, "We were tough little kids swimming in that hot water."

"I think people have adjusted fairly well to a bad situation," I said, and I remembered the old man, whose face was as round and his eyes were as bright as a barn owl's, who had been so good-natured about the tribulations of camp life.

Yoshio scowled. "The Nisei can shrug it off, but mark my words, the Issei will never get over the shame." He shuffled off.

Kiko got up to stretch her legs. "My mother hasn't adjusted well to the breakdown in our family. Yuki has the run of the camp, Tad joined the Army against my father's wishes, and I am living my life as I choose. My mother has learned a little English and I have learned more Japanese, and as a result we are much closer. She told me that she came to Seattle by boat with the last of the picture brides in the early Twenties. She was only eighteen when she met my father, who was much older, and she cried and wanted to return to Japan. That was impossible. The people in her prefecture were experiencing a famine and hers would be just another mouth to feed. It wasn't a love match, but my mother was always loyal to my father, even during the years when they were forced to live and raise us kids in a dilapidated hotel my father managed."

"Tadashi never told me about your mother being a picture bride."

"He probably doesn't know about it. At first I was embarrassed to learn that I was the result of an arranged marriage."

Tadashi and I had planned to honeymoon in Spokane and I would have taken the bus home. Instead, I prepared to leave the next morning with the Reverend and his wife. Kiko was there to say goodbye and to register one more complaint. "Can you imagine those soldiers hassling Tad about getting out of this place, and he was in uniform?"

I was apprehensive as I climbed the porch stairs of our house. I knew how they felt about my going to Idaho. Dad would sulk for a few days and refuse to talk to me. Mom would be sarcastic and try to make me feel guilty.

I found them sitting side by side on the davenport in the living room. They didn't greet me. They just stared searchingly.

"She's gone and done it. She's done it," Mom started to cry. "Shame on you. You couldn't wait, could you? We thought we had a daughter who would have waited for the proper young man and had a wedding that our relatives and friends could come to. You've cheated us out of our due, and you've cheated yourself."

"Girlie," and I knew that Dad was using that word to express his contempt, "you've got big ideas about equality between the sexes and the races. You'll learn a thing or two when you have to walk ten paces behind. You're a white Jap. You were determined to spoil your life and you've done it. I want no part of it. It's time for you to get out of my house. I don't want to see you again for a long, long time."

I tried to exit slowly and with dignity, but my body had been smashed into pieces and I had to pause to pick up my leg bones, my arm bones, and my head. Even though all my pieces were still connected, I felt disjointed by my parents' rejection and my ears rang with the erratic beat of my heart.

I made it to the hall and maneuvered the baggage of my disjointed body and suitcase through the front door, all the while expecting Mom to come running with apologies.

But no one followed me and I walked down the front steps to the street. As though on cue, the bus appeared from below the hill on Yesler Way and, as I stepped off the curb, it stopped and I climbed on.

19

I didn't know where I was going until the bus hit the long, steep hill that takes Yesler Way past the Smith Tower to Pioneer Square and the waterfront. There was only one place for me to go—the houseboat, where I could elaborate on my sad story and elicit Frannie's sympathy.

As I stepped onto the docks to which the houseboats are attached a dozen cats faded into the shadows. It was quiet except for the radios. I was relieved to see a light in Gina's and Frannie's floating home.

Frannie looked dowdy in her nightgown, her face swollen from crying, no mascara on her curled lashes, no dark red lipstick, not even a bobby pin or a ribbon in her soft brown hair.

I hid my shock with an ebullient outburst. "I've been banished. Dad doesn't want to see me again for a long, long time!"

I didn't expect a stony-faced response. I lowered my voice to a whisper. "What's the matter, Frannie? Did you fall for a second lieutenant at the Fort Lawton Officer's Club and now he's gone?" I regretted the barb immediately.

Frannie lurched at me. "Yes, Smarty, that's exactly what happened. It never occurred to me that he wouldn't write after he shipped out. And now I'm pregnant."

I felt a sharp pain in my stomach. Anger swept over me.

Frannie had watched me closely. "I should never tell you anything, Robin. You're like the rest of the family. You've acted superior for years because you thought I was boy crazy and you managed to keep a lid on your emotions."

My voice came out raggedly. "I'm sorry. We've been nasty to each other since we were little kids. It's time we stopped that."

We were silent for a long time and then Frannie exploded. "I'm a dead duck if anybody finds out about this! What's the matter with our family anyway? I hate their pettiness, their ugly jokes, and their self-righteousness. There's something mean about them, especially your Uncle Fritz."

"Grandma and your mother are exceptions," I reminded her.

"Of course, Mom and Grandmom are tops, but I'll get no support from them. I wouldn't dare tell them. Why is it so shameful to love someone?"

I offered Frannie the best explanation I could think of. "Puritanism. Kiko and Tadashi weren't brought up with intolerance, shame, and guilt like we were."

My mind struggled with the intricacies of family politics. Unlike our mothers who had never worked, Frannie and I had jobs, and our fathers, who were led to believe that it was their duty to protect us even when that meant making us afraid of everything, were alarmed by our growing independence. Feeling defeated, they got mad, lashed out at us, and rejected us.

"Your Uncle Fritz called me the streamlined kid and he didn't mean it as a compliment. What am I going to do? I've got to find my way out of this mess. I'd rather die than tell my parents."

"Let's quit our jobs. I'll take money out of the bank and we'll leave town. Blame it on me. Tell Aunt Vi I need a change and you're going along on this trip to keep me company."

"It'll never work."

"It has to work. We'll be good liars by the time this ordeal is over."

"Will wonders never cease? You'd spend your college money on me?"

"I won't let you ruin your life."

"Robin, you're right about not getting pushed into early marriage.

This is the wrong time for me to have kids. Two years from now, maybe, but not now."

"Goldie Mae lives in San Antonio. Tell Aunt Vi we're going down to visit Goldie Mae."

At first I found it exciting to contemplate the move, but the euphoria lasted a short time, fading like a photo print left in hypo overnight.

I dreaded giving notice to Dr. Noble, especially now that I was his secretary. Because I couldn't tell him the real reason for my quitting, he would think me frivolous and unpatriotic for leaving my job during wartime and a labor shortage.

I was surprised when he said to me, "I've been worried about you for a long time. If you were my daughter, I'd send you on an extended vacation. When you've had a good rest, come back and we'll try to fit you in."

On my last day at the War Labor Board, Marcelyn, Kathy, and Jane gave me a party with beautiful confections from the Swiss Pastry Shop.

When Frannie and I took the ferry to Indianola to say goodbye to Grandpa and Grandma, we found Grandpa sitting on a log outside the woodshed smoking a pipe.

"You still a pacifist?" he asked me.

"I think so."

"If we win this war—and Roosevelt thinks we will—we may have been saved by a narrow squeak." Grandpa blew a perfect smoke ring and watched it disintegrate above his head.

"Saved from what?"

"German technology. We're in a deadly race to build the biggest bomb."

It was a grey day, threatening rain. The remains of last summer's vegetable garden looked scraggly. Beyond that, the dark woods stood mute and dank. The only signs of life were the tiny bushtits flitting through the madrona tree and Grandma's bantams scratching for earwigs.

"The difference between you and me is that you hate killing and I hate injustice," Grandpa continued.

"I suppose you're going to say that now we have a new nobility to fight—the dictators?"

"Yes. Unfortunately, fighting for freedom is never-ending and little is accomplished without bloodshed."

"Then we'll always have war," I said gloomily.

"Maybe, maybe not." He pulled himself up, stooped for a load of wood, and headed for the kitchen.

Frannie made the announcement over lunch. "Robin and I are here to say goodbye. We've quit our jobs and are leaving for San Antonio to visit a friend. Who knows, maybe we'll stay until the war is over."

Grandpa and Grandma stared at us open-mouthed. "Do your parents approve of this?" Grandpa asked.

I wanted to say that Frannie and I were free, white, and twenty-one, but if I did, I'd sound just like Uncle Fritz. "I don't think it matters because Uncle Tolly and my father have kicked us out."

"But why?" Grandma had a stricken look.

"Frannie broke her curfew and I plan to marry Kiko's brother, Tadashi."

Dead silence prevailed. I saw the hurt in Grandma's eyes, remembering no doubt when Grandpa disowned Rose and Pansy, and now the same was happening all over again.

"Are you going to reject me, Grandpa?"

"No, of course he isn't!" Grandma exclaimed, looking rattled but determined. "We are stupid if we refuse to learn from the past. I hope you'll be happy, dear."

Later, Grandpa handed us envelopes. "This is for your meals on the train. Don't settle for a dry sandwich brought to your seat in a basket. You eat in the diner and enjoy the scenery over a linen tablecloth."

As we walked up the road to catch our ferry, we stopped just before we went out of sight of the house to wave and blow kisses. Grandpa and Grandma stood on the back porch, motionless, as though they had been caught in a snapshot.

We gave Nellie $30 to cover three months' rent of the houseboat and she agreed to watch the place until Gina and Adrian returned. I said goodbye to Mr. Scavenius, my piano teacher, and to my old friends, Mrs. Mangini and Mr. Swanberg. I didn't want to face Mom and Dad.

It was a big surprise when I opened the door to find Mom and Aunt Vi standing on our dock, looking out of place in high heels, gloves, and fancy hats. A big wave hit as they maneuvered the planks to our door. Now we would be fending off endless arguments.

"You're crazy, Robin," Mom cried. "If you need a vacation you can spend it at home. If you and Frances go traipsing around the country in wartime your father will say you're no better than camp followers."

"Mom, I've worked a forty-eight-hour week..."

"Fiddlesticks. I hope you know what you're doing. For one thing, you're taking Violet's only child away with you. If anything happens to her, the blame is on your head. You'll spend all your college money on this foolishness, I suppose. Well, don't expect any help from us on that score."

Violet, the younger sister who always followed in Mom's footsteps, looked uncomfortable. "I think you should know that Christopher is now stationed at Polebrook Airfield in Northhamptonshire. He'll be flying missions over Germany. Daisy is beside herself with worry, and now she'll be worrying about you too, dear."

Aunt Vi was the only one to see us off. As the train chugged out of King Street Station, she waved tearfully.

"Your mother is a darling," I said to Frannie. "Mine was standoffish when I tried to kiss her goodbye."

Frannie smiled. "By golly, I think we pulled it off."

20

Frannie and I nestled into our chairs on the all-night milk run to Portland, Oregon, too excited to sleep.

Behind us, a knobby-kneed girl, a character out of a John Steinbeck novel, sat with a tough-looking sailor who wore a gold earring in his left ear. It took a boy of ten to show the couples across the aisle how to turn two chairs around so they could play rummy in comfort. An old cowboy up front complained about someone trying to steal his jacket, which contained his false teeth. "That's the first time I've ever heard of anybody taking off with a fella's false teeth!" he guffawed.

Lights went out at ten o'clock in the chair cars and everybody settled down. The snores and snorts mingled with the piercing whistle of the panting locomotive. Outside, brush fires and the lights of little towns threw shadows across the sleepers, while clothing, hung from the luggage racks above the seats, undulated like dancing ghosts.

On our first morning Frannie and I warmed our hands on cups of bitter coffee served to us by the news butch. Later we struggled to keep upright in a lurching car while waiting in line for the diner. Periodically, orange peel, empty pop bottles, and paper litter were swept down the aisle as though we passengers were inmates of a zoo.

Out of Portland a mother of seven children hung a clock above her seat and carried a potty in a brown sack. Three of her brood sat on a soldier's lap, played with his Adam's apple, and screamed through tunnels.

From the millworks of Washington and the wool pulleries of Oregon, the train moved on to the wineries of California. At Sacramento sailors in a troop train on another track pantomimed wildly at the girls in our train. Everyone doubled up laughing at the antics of these GIs.

When I wasn't watching the people around me I stared out the window and dreamed about Tadashi. Frannie was more pensive.

"I'll bet your dad wouldn't kick Chris out if he married a Japanese girl," she said, puckering her mouth around a pencil over a crossword puzzle. "He wouldn't like it, but he'd put up with it."

The reminder made me angry. "I suppose they expect me to come crawling back. I'll never give Dad a chance to call me 'girlie' again. Why do women get the blame for everything? We should have the same opportunities as men. We're half the population and just as smart. We should be half the doctors, professors, and politicians in the world."

Frannie interrupted me with a small laugh. "That's silly, Robin. Women are the homemakers and they have to raise the children."

"Why? Why is it all up to women? Why is it that you never see a woman's face at peace negotiations? Don't you think women have something to offer at the conference table?"

Frannie looked bored. It was impossible to stir her into an argument, but Kiko's eyes would have been blazing by now. She and I wanted to change the world.

The world wasn't changing for the better very fast. I tried to comfort myself by thinking that people were fundamentally good, remembering the young woman who got on the train with two children—no baggage, no sweaters, no food, and probably no money. The children never complained, but the little boy coughed and everyone in the car seemed to worry about these three.

Two huge-handed Virginians watched the woman in a sloppy blouse and gaudy bandanna as she slept with mouth agape while her little boy raided other people's possessions.

143

"Pick those cakes off the floor before they get dirty," the older man said, grinning. His son watched in delight as the boy bounced somebody's orange down the aisle.

"I'm going to snatch you bald-headed," the younger man teased. "That man's going to git you. He'll cut your ears off."

The interest of everybody in the car centered on the boy and his mother as the train neared Oakland where the father supposedly waited. It was another mother, with four children quarantined for chicken pox in the only restroom with hot water, who gave the boy a scrub-down while he screamed his head off. Frannie and I filed off at Oakland with the others in our car, hoping to witness the reunion, but the father never showed up.

We were ill-tempered after sitting up two nights.

"What's wrong with having a crush on a boy?" Frannie demanded to know. "You always made me look frivolous."

"Because you swooned over every boy who came along. Your boyfriends wanted cars and your girlfriends fur coats. I thought all of you had shallow values."

"When you get on your high horse, Robin, you're obnoxious."

I decided Frannie was right. "I'm sorry that I was such a snob. In those days I believed that my life would be nothing after I married—no adventure, just boredom. I changed when I fell in love with Tadashi."

Having confessed this secret to Frannie made me realize that we had learned to trust each other. After a tempestuous childhood, we were friends at last.

It was a relief to change trains in Los Angeles. The station was like all other railway stations, jammed with GIs and women with babies and small children. Entire families were on the move, their household goods strapped to their backs. Redcaps darted through the crush of the crowd, the strings to their luggage tags flapping from their pockets like mops. Only Uncle Sam stood still, pointing a finger from posters, warning against discussing troop movements, ship sailings, and war equipment. In every station I heard what seemed like the same voice paging the same soldier: *"Calling Sergeant Jack Burke, Sergeant Jack Burke."*

After a layover in Los Angeles, we started the second half of our journey. Palm trees and orange groves changed to giant saguaros and marvelous sunsets in Arizona and New Mexico. The backs of our chairs were now vertical and hard. We were lured into the next car by the sound of an accordion and we joined in the singing.

A gunner's mate with twelve stars and four ribbons, who had survived being torpedoed several times, showed us a fist full of twenties and complained about not getting change for a telegram at Phoenix. We played rummy with soldiers from South Carolina and Georgia. When the game turned to poker, the men sat on their money whenever the MPs came through.

Frannie was sick after Los Angeles and stopped eating. I kept a paper sack handy just in case. Frannie, who primped before going for a walk on the beach at Indianola, was surrounded by young men and didn't care how she looked.

It was hot in Texas. We walked to the water dispenser in our anklets, leaving our shoes behind, and sat with our feet out the open windows.

I brooded over the family situation. If Uncle Tolly wanted to protect Frannie, why had he locked her out? If Dad really wanted to make me happy, why had he shunned me? Society imbued men with the idea that they are absolute monarchs, their women and children had to be obedient, and any disloyalty enraged them. Would Dad and I ever forgive each other?

Three different rail routes met in the frantically busy town of El Paso. It was exciting to wait in the station and hear the stationmaster call out the names of places to the north, east, and south. When the Atchison, Topeka and Santa Fe train went out, he called, "*Kansas City… Chicago… and all points East!*" The Southern Pacific was announced with calls for San Antonio and New Orl'ns. As we walked the platform beside another train, solemn faces looked down at us, and because of the strange feeling these men gave me and the big PW's on their shoulders, I knew they were German prisoners of war.

A train passed our car of open windows and someone yelled, "Where y'all goin'—New Orl'ns?" I heard snatches of conversation. "Look at that little bitty girl and that big old boy ... That mountain was big, and I mean it was big! ... You gonna carry me in your car? ... There's noth'n better'n a good politician and noth'n sorrier than a sorry one ... Y'all can tote and fetch, but I'm fixin' t'do different, I reckon ... There ain't but three of the boys who done got paid…"

A cowboy named Eddie explained to us, "Texans start out slow and then cut their words. Chicagoans talk even-like and clear, but faster. New Yorkers just jabber."

I wanted to know why I heard soldiers in the South exclaim "San Antone." Sometimes it was like a hello or an expletive. More often it was a sigh, the body saying wordlessly, "Please stop the war so I can go home." San Antone.

I felt the pulse of the nation and the beat was strong and steady. The American people were diverse and vigorous. This beautiful, wonderful country of mine was bound to win the war.

I was exuberant as I tried to express my feelings in a letter to Tadashi. Then I realized that the Negroes in our car had disappeared and was shocked to discover the laws for Texas and Louisiana posted between cars: "*Each compartment of a railroad coach,*" the notice read, "*divided by good and substantial wooden partitions with a door therein shall be deemed separate coach within the meaning of this law and each separate coach shall bear in some conspicuous place appropriate words in plain letters indicating the race for which it is set apart.*"

Disillusioned, I put the letter aside.

Frannie turned to me with a frown between her eyes. "If my father knew, he'd call me damaged goods."

I rose out of my chair, wagging a finger at her. "Don't use that ugly phrase. When this is over we'll go on with our lives as though nothing happened."

"Things will never be the same," murmured Frannie as she turned her face away from me.

⁂

There were more towns, more huge slabs of ice stowed away in bins below the cars, more orangeade and box lunches, more cacti, and more of never-ending Texas. Finally after over four days of travel, Frannie and I slid into San Antonio at 3:30 a.m.

After we gathered our luggage we settled down to wait for daylight. When people cleared out of the station I ran to a telephone booth to look up Goldie Mae. When I found no listing for her my spirits plunged.

Bombastic, irrepressible Goldie Mae. I saw her face, her blond ringlets springing, and heard her say, "I've been screwed, glued and tattooed."

I was scared. How could I manage in a strange city without her help?

21

When the city of San Antonio was awake and bustling, someone directed me to the USO Travelers' Aid Service where a lady at the housing desk gave me a listing that had just come in. "It's a few blocks from here. Just walk thatta-way." As I turned to go, I noticed a sign on the counter: Typist Wanted.

"I can type."

"Great," the housing lady said as she pulled out a form and handed it to me.

Miss Kilpatrick, the director of the agency, was tall and skinny with a face that intimidated rather than accommodated. After she had looked over my application, she said, "I hope you stay longer than the Army wives do. We pay $100 a month. I know that's less than half of what you've been getting but your money will go farther here than in Seattle, and we do give raises occasionally. We have a thirty-nine-hour week, seven hours daily and half-day on Saturday. Can we expect you next Monday at nine?"

I was elated as I left her office. I had been in San Antonio less than six hours and had a job already. Just around the corner from the USO Travelers' Aid, tucked in among modern buildings, was the Alamo. It could be exciting living here.

The address given me was for a huge old house surrounded by tall trees. A woman hanging clothes in the backyard wore only a slip with a green apron and was barefoot. Her grey hair framed an animated face with friendly blue eyes. She introduced herself as Mrs. Andlauer.

"I can tell you're from up north because you haven't learned to strip yet. Except when a norther blows down from Canada, it's hot here."

A mockingbird hopped to the ground from a low branch and a cardinal whizzed by. The cicadas in the trees were as noisy as lawnmowers.

Mrs. Andlauer showed me a room on the first floor. There were two cots, a small icebox, a hot plate, and shelves with two each of plates, cups, glasses, bowls, and pans. The cost was $8 per week. Frannie and I would share the first-floor bathroom with the Andlauers. Upstairs there were four large rooms occupied by couples from New York, Florida, Wyoming and Hawaii. The Andlauers' son occupied the tower room on the third floor.

"Bernard's going to be a concert pianist," Mrs. Andlauer said proudly. "Hear him? He's playing Beethoven's Sixth. He practices fifteen hours a day. Thank goodness, the Army didn't want him—he has an eye problem—but our other son is in the Navy."

Mrs. Andlauer seemed pleased to learn that my name was Mueller. "There's a large colony of Germans here. We came over twenty-one years ago. My husband was a professor and I was a ballet dancer in France when we met. Now he writes articles on economics and I teach ballet, French, and piano. I'm having a French class in the backyard this afternoon and you and your cousin are welcome to join us."

Mrs. Andlauer led me through living and dining areas cluttered with antiques, all the available wall space covered with huge oil paintings. There were two pianos in the living room, one in the hall, and another in a sunroom adjacent to the dining room. There were five pianos in the house, counting Bernard's in the tower room. An old-model Chickering was identical to one I'd seen in a museum.

I walked back to the station and returned by taxi with Frannie and the luggage. Frannie collapsed on one of the cots and fell asleep. I opened my two suitcases and let them sit. Soon we'd have to get ice for the icebox and food to cook on one burner, all in the presence of cockroaches and ants.

Upstairs a radio blared and between singing commercials and the war news a Chopin waltz floated down, sweet and reassuring. I went across the hall to the sunroom and, in the midst of wicker furniture and potted plants, tried the piano. It felt good to play again. When I finished the *Valse Caprice*, I whirled the stool around and came face to face with a young man whose eyes were bright and searching like those of the sharp-shinned hawk I'd rescued from a cat some months ago.

"I enjoyed that," he said, smiling.

"Do you practice on all the pianos?" I asked, knowing that this was Bernard.

"Yes, I like to play different instruments. My father's hobby is to keep them tuned."

I had pictured him in a tux, not expecting to see him in a loose, unbuttoned shirt, shorts, and barefoot like his mother.

"Someday I'd like to hear you play Rachmaninoff's *Concerto No. 3*."

Bernard swung his right arm in an arc and bowed. "Gladly, Madam, I'll play all your favorites any time, but when my mother's away, I play boogie woogie."

On the evening of our first day in San Antonio, Frannie and I ate dinner at a little neighborhood restaurant, recommended by Bernard, where we had calves' brains mixed with scrambled eggs, two vegetables, a tall glass of iced tea, and bread without butter, all for twenty-five cents apiece. For ten cents more we could have had Wiener schnitzel. Later, I bought eggs, bread, and juice for breakfast.

When I woke up the next morning, birds whistled, roosters crowed, and cicadas shrilled.

Bernard took us sightseeing to the Mission San Jose, built in 1731, which bore marks of siege from the time of the Alamo surrender. Huge century plants grew beside it. A group of Mexican women, hooded with black lace shawls, paused in the doorway. Four nuns ambled across the courtyard, dressed in white tunics with a wide, wine-colored band extending from neck to hem, their heads covered with black cloth.

Bernard escorted us along the River Walk. San Antonio was the Venice of the South, he said, and he explained how the WPA had landscaped the river with waterfalls and tropical plants before the war. He promised to bring us back on Thursday evenings for band concerts at the Arneson River Theater.

At the Alamo, I read a newspaper clipping of February 29, 1930, which quoted a journalist's interview with Mrs. Susannah Dickinson some fifty years earlier. She and her baby were the only white survivors of the Alamo massacre.

As much as I loved San Antonio for its white adobe buildings and green-shuttered houses, I was shocked to see that only rear seats on buses were available to colored patrons, and they were forced to use separate toilets and drinking fountains. When Frannie drank from the wrong fountain and was chastised by a policeman, she scowled in disgust.

Bernard's silky brown hair spilled over his forehead. He swept it back with long fingers as though he were playing arpeggios. "Negroes prepare and serve food to us at restaurants and take care of our children, but they aren't allowed to drink from our fountains. It's a way to subjugate them."

On my first day at the USO, the social workers were agitated like jam at rolling boil. Agnes, the Army wife from New York, explained, "Those two old ladies in the lobby are known to Travelers' Aid Societies all over the country. They save up for trips and when their money runs out TAS has to pay their way home."

I took dictation from the social workers and wrote up cases and filed them. I was stunned to learn that poor and hungry people roamed from state to state to work in the beets, the oranges, or whatever crop needed harvesting. Many of the Mexican laborers had tuberculosis or were malnourished. How could there be hunger in the United States of America?

The McKays traveled from crop to crop in an old car, which served as their home and was their refuge when Mrs. McKay gave birth to their only child. Neither had gone beyond the third grade. He herded sheep at night as a boy and she picked cotton until her stepfather ran her off at the age of twelve. I spotted this couple in the lobby and was struck by their sweetness and their innocence. At twenty-nine they were already stooped and wrinkled. Happily, the little social worker from Alabama found housing for the McKays and a job for him.

As chief letter writer, Frannie hit on the idea of referring to Mrs. Andlauer as Goldie Mae, which reinforced our story about going to San Antonio to visit her. I censored Frannie's letters to make sure we got our stories straight. We had to use caution in order not to arouse suspicion.

Tadashi's first letters were re-addressed at home, his neat printing dwarfed by Mom's scrawl. I could hear Mom say to Dad, "She's bound and determined to ruin her life."

It was no wonder that Tadashi didn't want me to join him in Tennessee. We wouldn't be able to walk down the street together much less find someone willing to marry us. Tadashi's outfit was battle ready, but orders to go overseas had not come through. He guessed that the big generals in Europe were reluctant to have Japanese-American soldiers under their command.

We had a big surprise when Gina wrote from Hot Springs, Arkansas. She had been with Adrian in North Carolina while he recovered from war injuries, and now they were visiting his family and planning to leave soon for the little houseboat in Seattle. They wanted to stop in San Antonio to see us. "And that isn't all," Gina wrote. "Stony and Tyler are here on furlough and will accompany us as far as San Francisco. Rumor is that they are shipping out to Burma or China to service airplanes. After twenty months in Alaska, they'd go anywhere."

Frannie wilted when she heard the news. "I can't see them—you know that."

"Frannie, you don't show yet. You've got to see them. Just don't spill anything to Gina."

Stony was the first off the train early Sunday morning. He bounded off, picked me up and twirled me in a full circle. "You look good!" he cried. The freckle-faced kid with curly red hair was now a pale, thin man with hefty shoulders.

I heard Frannie say, "And you were tucked up there God knows where doing heaven knows what?"

We watched Adrian one-step off the train. When I embraced him he cautioned me, "Don't squeeze me too hard."

"The doctors didn't get all the shrapnel out," Gina explained.

We stood in a circle and grinned at each other. "Who would have dreamed we'd get together again in San Antonio of all places," Gina clucked happily, face beaming.

"Let's spend the day at Brackenridge Park," Stony suggested. "I haven't seen that place since I was a kid."

After the taxi delivered us, we rode through the zoo in mule carts and took ten-cent rides on the elephants.

Down in the pit with the three elephants, a trunk with two pink nostrils moved searchingly around my face. I aimed a peanut at close range and the elephant caught it, curved its trunk to its mouth and crunched.

"You're doing it all wrong," Stony said. "Say 'trunk up.'" The elephant opened its mouth wide and held its trunk in the air while Stony delivered a handful of peanuts into its mouth.

Next we went to the reptile garden for the rattlesnake fry. I turned my head when they killed the snake and refused to sample it. "You're missing something," Stony said. "It's kinda bony, but it's tasty, like half-fish and half-chicken."

We sat on a bench eating hot dogs. I asked Stony if he still hated the Army. "Hell, yes! All we do is sweat out chow lines and pick up cigarette butts. A lot of guys couldn't cope with the long, dark winter months in Alaska and committed suicide. We Arkansas boys took care of each other. I nearly got married on my furlough, but my girl got cold feet. Maybe she'll wait for me, maybe she won't."

The others joined us and Tyler turned to me. "Robin, Gina says you took the call about the bombing at Dutch Harbor, Alaska, nine months before the news hit the papers. We stood outside our Quonset huts and watched the dog fights." He turned to Adrian. "The Japanese evacuated Kiska a day before our forces landed, yet seven of our officers were killed."

Were they killed by their own men, I wondered?

"The Army sent the Seventh Infantry onto Attu in January—men trained for desert warfare with no arctic clothing. The nurses at the hospital in Anchorage were madder'n hell when those guys came in with frozen feet."

"They had orders not to take prisoners on Attu. Army Intelligence was furious because there was no one left to interrogate."

I poked Tyler. "They killed their Japanese prisoners?" He nodded.

"We had Aleuts, Eskimos, and Indians on Attu, acting as scouts for the Army behind Japanese lines, and when our forces landed and the scouts ran down to the beach to greet them the Seventh Infantry mowed them down."

I felt a sudden soreness in my throat and a dull ache in my eyes.

Adrian interrupted Stony and Tyler's report on events in Alaska. "We heard that Navy and Army brass were laying bets on which branch of service would take Attu. Same rivalry between Montgomery and Patton."

I had heard enough. I walked away and Gina and Frannie followed me.

"I hate that war talk," Gina said. "That's all I've heard since the boys got together. Adrian told me that when they landed on Sicily they sent in green troops—a bunch of eighteen-year-old kids—and the Germans shot them down one by one. Those kids were crying and screaming for their mothers."

After a moment or two Gina turned to us with a smile. "Say, when are you girls coming home?"

22

I burst into tears the day Mrs. Andlauer confronted me about Frannie.

"Frances is pregnant, is she not? Did you girls run away from home?"

I don't remember what I said, but I blubbered away about our fathers—how Frannie's had locked her out and mine was mad because I wanted to marry a Japanese boy.

"From what you tell me I can imagine how they'd react to an out-of-wedlock pregnancy. I may have a German name, but I am French. The French are forthright and realistic about such things. Falling in love is as natural as breathing, certainly not what I would call a sin. Americans have ridiculously Victorian and Puritanical views on sex. Imagine a girl having to sneak off to have a baby when she is most in need of family support." Mrs. Andlauer shook her head sadly. "When is she due?"

"In June."

"Have you found a good doctor? She should be seeing one every month and walking two miles a day. Because it's hard for you to get away from work, I'll have Bernard take us to my doctor. You must talk to someone at your agency. Frances needs help and the baby will need a home."

I felt completely unglued when I told Frannie about my conversation with our landlady. "Forgive me, Frannie, for being so inept. I've really let you down."

"What are you talking about, silly girl? When you came to the houseboat

I was contemplating suicide, trying to get up my nerve to jump off the Aurora Bridge. I knew I'd rather die than face my parents. In two minutes you came up with the solution to my problem. You gave up a good job to come here and now you're supporting me."

Fortified by Frannie's kind words, I arranged to see Miss Kilpatrick the next day. The stenographers hated her and the social workers complained that she made decisions instantly and without benefit of other people's opinions and supervised down to the smallest detail. In spite of her shrill and commanding voice and the eyes, which were as expressive as a parrot's, only sharper, there had to be a heart in Miss Kilpatrick's body. I had observed that she was tough with her employees, but she stood up for her clients and never looked down on them because they were poor or uneducated.

"Bring your cousin to see me. Many girls want to keep their babies, but we advise against it. There are families eager to adopt and we'll find a good home for this one. I want you to open a file in your cousin's name and I'll keep it on my desk. I'll dictate my notes directly to you and in that way we'll keep this secret between us."

"Our parents would be horrified if they knew, and they'd blame Frannie."

Miss Kilpatrick nodded. "Include that in the write-up."

Grandma would have said that Frannie looked "peak-ed." She was pale after sitting in our room all day reading novels and women's magazines. Without mascara and lipstick, she had a fragile quality that I thought was most appealing. I liked her hair hanging loose better than when it was tight with a permanent.

Frannie's spirits lifted after her talk with Miss Kilpatrick. "As soon as I get out of this fix, I'm going to get a job and pay you back your college money."

"I'll probably never go," I said.

"Don't say that. It's not an impossible dream. Yvonne got through four years on less than a thousand dollars."

Frannie now had Miss Kilpatrick and Mrs. Andlauer looking after her and I rejoiced for the lesser burden, but I felt weary from worry over Tadashi and Chris.

Christmas turned out better than we had expected. Frannie, Bernard and I were invited upstairs to the Coniglios' apartment where we spent Christmas Eve with the Army couples. The next day everyone joined the Andlauers for a potluck dinner. We were too busy to be homesick. The highlight of that day was the delivery by two Red Cross ladies of a dozen roses for me from Tadashi.

His letters stopped abruptly after Christmas with no warning that he might be shipping out. The entire month of January 1944 was a loss. The first week of February a letter finally arrived with an APO number on the envelope.

We had worked out a code system to get past the censor. Without it, I would not have known that he had landed in Italy. One of his little drawings told me so. By mentioning daisies in a field, I knew he was trying to tell me something, but I didn't know what.

"Looks like he'll be tangling with Hitler's storm troopers, the pick of the German army," Dr. Andlauer commented.

Tadashi never wrote about the war. Instead he described people in his outfit, such as the chaplain whose best friend was an atheist. The chaplain said of his friend, "He'd rather argue than eat." Now Tadashi wrote about German prisoners who were amazed to see Japanese-Americans in Europe.

In four months of being away I had not received a single letter from Mom. Aunt Vi relayed the news along with our ration books. Dad and Uncle Fritz were air wardens and Chris flew B-17s over Germany. Frannie's friend, Delaine, was also in England with her WAC unit having arrived in November 1943 shortly before the Little Blitz bombings started.

Mom was bitter with the knowledge that the British sent their airmen on night raids while U.S. Air Force officers—at least for the first few months—were flying in the daytime when the Germans could easily spot them and shoot them down. Unable to cope with the worry and the long days at home, Mom had actually gone to work for Boeing.

"Daisy's got a job!!" Aunt Vi wrote, and we knew by the exclamation points that both she and Mom were thrilled about it. "Daisy says that almost half of Boeing's total workforce is female. They have three shifts a day, seven days a week, and most employees are on a ten-hour day. She'll be working on holidays. Imagine!"

Gina and Adrian were happily settled in the houseboat on Lake Union. "Adrian has a job and loves being a civilian," Gina wrote, "although the adjustment to civilian life isn't easy. A guy has to do it alone and not in the company of other GIs as in boot camp."

I heard from David Engstrom occasionally. He served at a mental hospital in New England. While on a vacation trip he and other conscientious objectors tried to build decent outhouses for poor Negroes and were chased out of Florida.

Frannie never mentioned the man who had gotten her pregnant. I knew that she was deeply hurt, having loved someone who shipped out without saying goodbye or leaving a forwarding address.

Sometimes she complained about our family. "They're a bunch of prudes," she said one day. "Our mothers were too embarrassed to tell us anything. I knew girls in high school who didn't know where babies came from. Luckily for us, we had Yvonne, Delaine's sister, who was taking Sociology at the U. She educated us all right."

I thought about the pamphlets Frannie had slipped to me, which I hid under a board in my closet. "I think there's a conspiracy to keep girls as ignorant as possible."

Frannie objected. "The boys were ignorant too, but they talked to each other more than we did."

Spring slid by, March to May. Now it was June, time for Frannie to deliver. Bernard had thoughtfully parked the car at the curb, anticipating a midnight dash to the hospital. Everyone in the big house was asleep when we escorted Frannie down the walk dappled with the shadow of leaves caught in the moonlight, the stillness broken only by insects whirring, owls hooting, and an occasional howling dog.

After we arrived at the hospital Frannie was whisked away, and when I tried to follow her I was pushed into an office and handed forms and a pen. When I finished filling them out the clerk scrutinized the papers.

"Is your cousin married? We need to have the father's name. How do you plan to pay this bill?"

The unfriendliness aggravated my worry over a shrinking college fund. Did this woman see me as being too young to pay my bills? Many people were prejudiced against the young. Was I guilty of prejudice? I had thought pregnancy outside of marriage happened only to lower-class women. So, I was wrong. No one should be regarded as lower class. People deserve respect regardless of their station in life.

It was as though I was talking to Tadashi and I could hear him gently expressing his dissent. "You think Hitler and Mussolini deserve respect?" Tadashi believed that prejudice was all-pervasive, part of the human condition, irremediable. Everyone looked down on someone for some reason. When they acted on their prejudice and discriminated, that's when things got ugly.

When I joined Bernard in the waiting room, by way of a hall clogged with patients in wheelchairs and stretched out on makeshift beds, I sat next to a fan that blew warm air in my face. Perspiration ran down my back. In Texas, in or out of the shower, I was wet all the time.

I felt myself slip into sleep. When I awoke it was daylight and Mrs. Andlauer was leaning over me. "Frances had her baby and it's a boy. She's sleeping now, but the baby's in the nursery. I want to see him."

I was surprised to find the door to the nursery open with only a young Mexican girl in attendance. The girl picked up Frannie's baby and placed him in my arms. I was electrified when I felt the warm bundle wiggle. When I looked down at him I had the amazing feeling that everything this baby would be some day was already squeezed into that tiny body. This little guy was sure of himself, he knew exactly where he was going, and he was already on his way.

"I name him Skeezix," I announced as I returned him to his crib. He clung to Bernard's finger. He sneezed, he frowned, and he yawned. He was so tiny for all that.

Mrs. Andlauer removed his blanket, his shirt, and diaper. "Some day Frances will want to know about him and we'll be able to tell her that he's perfect." She turned him on his stomach and he looked like a little frog ready to jump to the floor and out the open window.

Later, Miss Kilpatrick informed me that the adoption agency had picked up the baby and delivered him to his new parents who were so delighted with him that they offered to pay for Frannie's hospital stay. I felt a tug of remorse because Skeezix was gone and I would never see him again.

When I visited Frannie, she faced the wall, eyes red. A young nurse tried to cheer her up. As she gave Frannie a shot she winked at me. "I give so many shots that people's posteriors look like faces to me."

When we were alone Frannie leaned close to me so that other women in the ward couldn't hear. "My body doesn't belong to me anymore. Those horrible people in the delivery room treated me like an automobile on an assembly line."

In the days that followed I hugged her a lot. Finally came the day when she painted her fingernails and toenails red, curled her eyelashes and applied mascara, and pressed her best dress. That same day she found a job as cook's helper at a Mexican restaurant on the River Walk.

23

While Frannie was in the hospital, the Allies captured Rome and the invasion of France began under General Eisenhower. Dr. Andlauer said that D-Day had occurred, a spectacular event that enabled the allies to land in Normandy. Life was a slow, painful grind in pursuit of victory.

It was a hot summer. I was thirsty all the time and drank gallons of Lime Rickeys and Dr. Peppers and longed for Seattle water, which burst out deliciously cold from the faucet, having come straight from the Cascade Mountains. Thanks to Mrs. Andlauer, a small electric icebox was installed in our room.

After working in an air-conditioned office, stepping out into the street was like entering a furnace. On my way past the Alamo my heels sank into the soft asphalt. An artesian well was being drilled under the Gunter Hotel and the constant din of construction filled the hot air. Evenings, I read and caught a phrase or two of Mozart from Bernard's tower room, while the Army couples upstairs stomped back and forth, laughing and hollering, their radios blaring.

I missed evenings in Seattle where city lights blazed in the clear, crisp atmosphere of winter, and in summer people rushed home as though they were headed for a picnic. In the Pacific Northwest a sunny day following a rainy one was like a holiday.

But I loved Texas too. There was something about the blueness of the sky that was different from any blue I'd ever seen before, especially the blue behind a row of white houses after the sun had gone down. I'll never forget the rapid turn of a windmill in the warm breeze, people with fliivers, bicycles, and an old black baby buggy, loading up at ice houses on the main roads; and those who sat in their yards and on porches with babies and pitchers of lemonade, ice clinking in their glasses.

On my way to work I saw cows being led to pasture along a busy arterial, chickens running loose in front yards, and ducks perched on curbs. San Antonio was overrun with crickets in September 1944. One went into hiding in our room and could be heard at all hours.

The November election was imminent. One neighbor believed that if Dewey were elected president he would be at a disadvantage with Churchill and Stalin. Mrs. Green, who lived across the street, didn't know anything about politics, she said, except what her husband told her, and that was too much. He said Roosevelt had ruined the country.

Mrs. Green went on to say, "I heard they're going to let the niggers vote this year. They may be doing away with the $1.75-a-year poll tax. Some states don't have poll taxes, they tell me."

Now twenty-one, I looked forward to casting my first vote.

It was hard to get film, but Bernard's friend in the photography business promised to keep me supplied. I borrowed Bernard's camera and his bicycle and headed for the country. When I returned, I'd shot three rolls of film.

Bernard was there when I spread the black and white prints on the table in the sunroom. "Look, Robin, you caught the ball in mid-air!" he said of the picture of a toddler sitting on a curb wearing his father's cowboy hat and watching three older boys play ball. "You've got a flair for taking pictures."

I had snapped two nuns as they paused long enough for one to lift her skirt. Perhaps she showed her companion a new pair of shoes. It was a touching photograph, I thought, because the nuns were young enough to yearn for pretty things that were denied them.

I bought a small leather-bound album and when my four favorite pictures were enlarged I cropped them and pasted them in. I could carry the album in my purse and take it out now and then for a look.

The expeditions revived me. Tadashi was right. Make quilts. Write poetry. Creating something made me happy. While I scoured for pictures, I forgot the war for a little while.

During the hottest part of the summer, Frannie and I lay on our cots and dreamed about home.

"I wish I had a piece of Grandma's prune küchen right now," I said, envisioning the huge cookie sheets, fresh prunes halved and laid out in long rows of little fruit faces on white dough drizzled with sugar and cinnamon.

"How about a slice of her gooseberry pie?" Frannie lay on her cot in bra and panties.

"I'd settle for a cup of her dried cherries. How does she find time to pit them and cut out all the bird pecks?"

Indeed, how did she find the energy to prepare those big platters of cherries I'd seen drying in the conservatory? It took tons to fill a jar or two. How unconscionably her granddaughters had raided the pantry, carrying off fists full of that precious fruit.

Frannie propped herself up on one elbow. "Remember the shrub Grandma made of raspberries and vinegar stored in that big stone jar, weighted down with a plate? I didn't like it much."

I grinned at Frannie. "It wasn't bad with lemonade, but I like Grandpa's blackberry wine better. We had a gallon of it in the pantry and I had a sip or two every day after school."

"I wonder if she still makes parched corn. How did our teeth survive that hard stuff? And remember how your mother sprinkled sugar on our lettuce to get us to eat it?"

When we were at Indianola Grandma made custards and baked potatoes for our lunch. We loved her concoction of hamburger, onions and tomatoes with all her leftovers thrown in. Everyone called it "Grandma's mystery." Nothing went to waste in that house.

Did our mothers miss us? In Frannie's Wallingford house and my house on Yesler Way, there was a picture enlarged from a snapshot, tinted and framed, which caught us on scooters, bloomers showing, our hair cut in identical Dutch bobs. "So cute," our mothers always said.

One Sunday Dr. Andlauer appeared at our door. A handsome man with abundant grey hair, smooth red cheeks and a goatee, he smelled of Prince Albert tobacco and Burma Shave. He held a telegram, which he said was addressed to both of us. Frannie and I exchanged alarmed glances. Someone had died. Was it Grandpa or Grandma? Could it be one of our dads or moms?

Frannie tore the envelope apart and I saw her face crumple. "Oh, Robin, it's Chris. He was shot down over Germany."

We collapsed into chairs and remained immobile for hours trying to absorb the shock of knowing that Chris, who had been with us all our lives, was gone now, never to return.

We called home from a telephone office that specialized in long distance calls for men and women in service. Frannie placed the call and Aunt Vi answered. When Frannie handed me the receiver, I heard Mom's voice, distant and cold, her words like taut rubber bands zinging, automatically repeating what she must have said to neighbors, friends and distant relatives.

I longed to hear Mom say, "We miss you, honey." Instead, she sounded annoyed when she ended our conversation with: "You shouldn't be gallivanting around the country at a time like this." Poor Mom.

We were gloomily silent on our way back to the Andlauers' house. We stopped at a drugstore where we watched a soda jerk fill our glasses with ice, cola, and cherry syrup. At the small table our heads touched as we bent over our drinks.

"I want to go home!" Frannie suddenly exclaimed.

"Go ahead. No one's stopping you."

"I won't go without you."

"You'll have a long wait." I took a deep breath, knowing I was on the brink of a confession. "Remember when Mom glowered at us and said we had to be ladylike and mind our p's and q's? We didn't know what we'd done wrong, but I had a feeling about it. I was convinced that it was shameful to be female and that my body was ugly. I hated being a girl. I was envious of Chris, and now that he's gone, I feel guilty for all that. Poor Dad. He dreamed of Chris making his fortune in South America."

Frannie nodded sympathetically. "If your mother expected you to marry a swanky guy, she didn't build up your confidence any. Aunt Daisy was always knocking you down."

"It isn't just Mom. All my life, Dad has denigrated my triumphs with, 'She's doing okay… for a girl.' And I've got to learn how to handle Uncle Fritz with his talk about wops and chinks, darkies, and pinkos."

"Robin, you're going to have to forgive your folks some day."

Later, as we lay on the grass in the backyard, Frannie dug up memories of Chris. "Remember when Chris and his buddies were naked out on that raft, and we hid their clothes? That was the summer when we couldn't sunbathe on the spit at the head of Miller's Bay because of a dead cow. I found a dugout and inside was a spinal column with ribs and hair attached. When I told everybody about it, they laughed at me. Your dad called it a cock and bull story. Before I could prove it, a fire broke out in the driftwood and burned the entire end of the spit. Well, Chris walked out there before the fire and verified my story, but no one believed him either."

On the Fourth of July, Frannie and I had to be satisfied with Roman candles, spit devils, and sparklers, but Chris got to set off homemade bombs in tin cans.

"He was a good brother," I said in a low voice. "When I was little, he carried me home when I got hurt. He never answered my letters, but he sent me presents from New York."

I stared at the stars while hot tears streamed down my cheeks and into my ears.

Poor Chris. I thought only girls were poured into molds, but boys were also. "Don't cry. Be a man." From the time he was a little boy, society had prepared him for the ultimate betrayal—war. What was it like when your plane plunged to the earth and you knew you were going to die—at age twenty-four?

Frannie and I remained outside until after midnight. Then we went back to our room and lay on our cots while the lace curtains swayed in the warm breeze.

24

Tadashi wrote that the 100th Infantry Unit, made up of Hawaiian-born Japanese-Americans, and the 442nd Regimental Combat Team, composed of mainland Nisei, became a single family in June 1944. That's when he met Japanese from Hawaii.

"They talk in Pidgin English, play ukuleles, and swing their hips in large circles when they dance. They never cease to amaze us. I tried to get a B for Buddhist stamped on my dog tags, but no one would do it."

Kiko wrote that one of Tadashi's friends had come home wounded from service in Italy, and he had told her that the Atlantic crossing took twenty-eight days in a convoy so large that they never saw the outer edges of it. Now I knew what Tadashi wanted to tell me when he mentioned daisies in a field.

By October Tadashi's letters were shorter, sweeter and more serious. "My father says the chance of being born into this world is so rare that we should be filled with gratitude. I am grateful for being a part of your life and for your being a part of mine."

I tried to write to him every day, seizing on anything that might interest him, at the same time feeling inadequate about my trivial accounts. Did he remember in 1928, when we were both five years old, seeing airplanes sent out to announce the presidential winner? Most people couldn't afford radios, so green lights on the planes let them know that Herbert

Hoover had won the election. And someone had told me that I had an accent. I wrote a sketch about the Negro who polished shoes in the lobby of our building and had all his teeth covered with gold. I wrote about an incident that happened one day on a bus. A girl poked a lady wearing a big hat to offer her a seat. When the lady turned around, she was a Negro. The Southern girl was embarrassed. "They'll think I'm a Northerner," I heard her say. I sent all my letters to Tadashi by eight-cent airmail rather than by three-cent regular mail.

Tadashi's letters had dribbled to nothing by the middle of October. I lay awake unable to sleep. Was he on a battlefield somewhere? Did he have to go for days without a bath or change of clothes? Was he cold and wet? Did he have to sleep in the open without cover? Was he hungry?

One night I dreamed about the eighteen-year-old soldiers shot down in the landing on Sicily. Their sandbag bodies sprouted wiry limbs and they all wore sad, white faces. As they shuffled off, the last one to go turned to me with a white, smiling mask such as Tadashi had worn at my first Bon Odori in 1938, the summer before our sophomore year.

When I discovered the little frog missing from my lily-pad ring, I tore off all the bedding and ran my hands over the bare floor, frantically searching for it.

Frannie forced me into a chair. "You could look high and low and never find it," she scolded as she made up my bed. "Some day a jeweler will make you a new frog. You're worried about Tadashi, but you aren't going to help him by getting sick."

Kiko's telegram came the second week of November. I was alerted when returning from work I saw Frannie, Bernard and Mrs. Andlauer standing on the porch. It was as though one of them had spotted me and said, "Here she comes now," and the other two deliberately refrained from glancing in my direction. Frannie looked tearful and apologetic when she surrendered the telegram.

Without a word I walked to the door of our room, sat down on my cot, and opened the yellow envelope. Tadashi had died on October 31st in the Vosges Mountains near the town of Bruyeres in southern France.

I rolled up into a ball on my cot. I was hot and I wanted to be cool. A long-forgotten memory stirred of a little girl who, sick with pneumonia, had crawled under the porch and found comfort on the cold ground. When they found me, I had not wanted to be rescued.

"Is there anything I can do?" Frannie hovered over me, removing my shoes. She brought me dinner, but I could not eat.

I heard the clatter of dishes being put in the cupboards upstairs, the bang of the garbage can lid, and the slam of the back door. The radios swallowed up what remained of silence in the house.

It was nearly midnight before the big house was quiet. I summoned the image of Tadashi and there he was, eyes bright and mouth sweet with that special smile. How could he be dead when he was so alive in my mind?

I swallowed a sob and it caught like an inflated balloon in my throat.

After a long night, I lay quietly on my back staring at the ceiling, my eyes caught by a fly that flew in rectangles and squared off corners like a drum major.

Frannie fussed over me. "I phoned Miss Kilpatrick that you wouldn't be in today. Look what the girls sent you." She arranged the flowers in a mayonnaise jar. I glanced at the card. Everyone at the agency had signed with first names, even the social workers, who usually distanced themselves from the stenographers, even Cora Kilpatrick.

When I went back to work, all the employees of USO TAS, including the cleaning woman, stopped by my desk. Dry-eyed, I watched them as they stumbled through their condolences. Marooned in a void, my body novacained like a giant tooth, I plowed through the days that followed, typing letters and case histories. Evenings, I lay on my cot for hours without stirring.

"We are worried about you," Frannie confided. "Mrs. Andlauer says that you are bottling up your emotions and that isn't good for you."

I didn't care. I had lost my future. There would be no apartment overlooking the Ave for Tadashi and me, no walking across campus to classes together.

❀

The morning Miss Kilpatrick invited me into her office and nudged me into her client's chair, I felt myself spiraling down into a murky world. I was surprised to hear her say, "I lost my sweetheart in the last war. He was washed off his ship."

Dad would have said that this old maid was ugly as a mud fence but in that moment, I saw her as she must have been twenty-five years ago.

Mom had not written to me about Tadashi, and that hurt so much that I spilled over to Miss Kilpatrick. "I've been told in so many ways that I'm worthless. Mom must wish that I had died instead of Chris."

"Your mother is an angry woman. Her generation and mine won the vote. It was yours that won the right to work. We were dependent on our men and had limited opportunities. You aren't to blame for that."

"Mom says that another depression will engulf us after the war is over and I will be jobless. Will I be able to support myself? I don't want to live with my parents or spend my middle years punching a typewriter for a small wage."

"Women won't give up their independence. Thank goodness for that. I've seen too many single women trying desperately to feed hungry children."

"I don't want to go on living," I heard myself say and I knew that I had hit bottom. "I don't want to live in a world where every mouth is a slaughterhouse, where animals are in constant fear of being gobbled up, where humans are devoured by the little mouths we can't see. This life is poverty, greed, and war."

"Yes, this is a tough world," Miss Kilpatrick agreed, but she didn't coddle me. "You'll do all right," she said as she ushered me out. "You've got grit."

❀

One evening Sergeant Coniglio appeared at our door. "Robin, I want you to come upstairs to meet someone." I followed him to the big room that served as living room, bedroom, and kitchen for him and his wife.

As I sat down opposite a man in a wheelchair, whose Army jacket displayed his ribbons for service overseas, Mrs. Coniglio brought me a cup of coffee.

"I apologize for not getting up," the man said as we were introduced. "I've lost my feet and the Army hasn't replaced them yet." My confusion seemed to amuse him.

"Trench feet," Sergeant Coniglio hurried to explain. "Sergeant Larson is temporarily hospitalized at Fort Sam Houston and will be mustered out soon."

I tried not to look, but a quick glance revealed two rounded stubs jutting out from the man's rolled up pants. A hot, prickling sensation flashed across my upper arms and back.

Larson had sandy hair the color of his weathered face. I guessed that he was an old Army man in service before the war began, and at least thirty years old.

"Coniglio tells me your boyfriend was with the 442nd Regimental Combat Team." Larson drained his cup and signaled Mrs. Coniglio for more. "Those little guys are great fighters. If it wasn't for them, I wouldn't be here today."

I bristled. Those little guys, indeed!

"Have you heard of the Lost Battalion?" Sgt. Coniglio asked. "Larson was with the Texas volunteers who got stuck behind enemy lines." I shook my head.

"The Japs freed us. They took some of the toughest fighting of the war. When was your boyfriend killed?"

"October 31st."

"He was in the rescue then. Those little iron men arrived late afternoon of the 30th. We popped out of our foxholes in a state of ecstasy, threw down our guns, and hugged them."

I tried to picture Tadashi being hugged by this man.

"They used everybody for our rescue," Larson said proudly. "That included the three battalions of the 442nd. Even the cook was on the line. Members of our 36th Division were amazed to see Orientals in American uniform."

"What happened the next day?" I asked.

"My feet were so swollen I couldn't get my boots on and they had to carry me out." I could see Tadashi as stretcher-bearer. Larson frowned as though he were reliving that ordeal. "Those pine forests in the Vosges Mountains were thick, dark, and spooky, and the wind made a wailing sound. It was rainy and cold, and by October we'd had snow."

I tried to visualize the place but could not. My head ached from staring at Larson with wide unblinking eyes.

Coniglio, who had been stateside all through the war, listened attentively. Larson turned to him. "And the Germans were everywhere with heavy artillery, machine guns, booby traps, snipers, mortar fire, and screaming meemies. They had nonmetallic mines that escaped mine detectors. The Bouncing Bettys and tree bursts exploded with terrible force. German artillery flew first and then we'd hear the gun go off, just the opposite of ours. Their machine guns went b-r-r-p; ours went putt-putt-putt. Life can never be the same after you've seen your buddy's head blown off, or you stop to check the body of a German soldier and he turns out to be a sixteen-year-old kid."

I held my breath. I didn't flinch.

"We had a major general who would have made a good football coach," Larson continued. "He kept telling us to advance, push harder, go, go, go. Even when we knew he was wrong we had to obey. That's how we got hung up behind enemy lines, surrounded by Germans, and fast running out of ammo, food, and medical supplies."

"Did the same general send the 442nd on the rescue mission?" I asked.

"Yes, the same. I heard later that the 442nd suffered over eight hundred casualties on that mission."

"How many Texans were rescued?"

"Out of two hundred and seventy-five of us, two hundred eleven got rescued."

I was shocked. "That's four times more dead and wounded than men rescued!"

"You can't allow a battalion to get surrounded and do nothing about it," Sergeant Coniglio explained. He and Larson smiled indulgently at me.

"Even if an equal or greater number of men are wiped out?"

There was no change in the expressions on the two sergeants' faces. They probably considered themselves too polite to argue with a woman. It was plain to me that the major general had needlessly sacrificed lives, including Tadashi's. Would he have sent hundreds to rescue members of the 442nd?

"You can be proud of your boyfriend, Ma'am. If he was like the others, he was a good fighter."

Tears spilled down my cheeks. "Are you okay?" Coniglio asked, sitting upright.

I jumped up and started for the open door. Coniglio grabbed me. "There... there," he said soothingly.

I broke away and stumbled into the hall. Mrs. Coniglio yelled at her husband. "What have you done to her?" And he bellowed back, "I haven't done anything. I thought she'd like to know that her boyfriend was a hero."

I had created a commotion. The other Army couples peered out their open doors and Bernard hurried down his narrow stairs. As I reached for the banister, I saw the Andlauers and Frannie looking up at me.

I bumped into Dr. Andlauer at the bottom of the stairs and he tried to hug me, but I pushed past him into my room and onto my cot, which was the only refuge I had.

25

Early in 1945, Kiko announced her engagement to Kenjiro, a Bainbridge Islander whom she had met at Minidoka.

"I won't be going back to school, Robin, because Kenji and I are starting a landscaping business. Having spent the last two and a half years reading books, I think I've gotten the equivalent of a college education, and social work has lost its appeal for me.

"My only regret is that I didn't seek employment in Chicago or New York many months ago when the War Relocation Authority allowed internees to leave camp, but with Tadashi in the service I felt obliged to stay with my family. The WRA kept tabs on everyone who left camp, of course, but the agency also helped place them in jobs. We were told that the farther east they went, the less hostility they encountered. I'm sure a lot of those Japanese will not return to the West Coast. Old Nihon Machi on Jackson Street will never be the same.

"Now that the ban is lifted and we are free to come back to Seattle, my father is reluctant to leave camp. He is worried about making a fresh start in a hostile environment. Uncle Daisho and Aunt Kazzie are worried too, because farmers in the valley have organized to discourage Japanese from returning. It's going to be hard.

"I was glad when the U.S. Supreme Court ruled that internment of the Japanese as a group could no longer be upheld. My faith in our Government was revived. Perhaps that will be as close to an apology as we'll ever get. Kenji says that ten people have been indicted for spying for Japan and all of them are Caucasian.

"Robin, when are you coming home? I want you to be there, waiting for us when we return."

Gina wrote that Nellie had bought another house and planned to live in it while she remodeled. "She wants to rent the houseboat to you for $10 a month. You'd better grab it. It's next to impossible to find housing in Seattle."

"I'm ready to go home," I announced to Frannie, expecting her to shout "Yippee!" Instead she was silent, lying on her cot with her shoes kicked off and a half smile on her face.

"You'll have to go by yourself, Robin, because I am staying in San Antonio. Bernard and I are getting married."

Now I understood why Bernard insisted on picking Frannie up each night and bringing her safely home from work, and why they were always late. I had been too tangled up with my grief and self-pity to observe the signs of a budding romance.

"Where are you going to live?" I asked.

"New York. Bernard has the promise of a job with the symphony after the war is over. Dr. Andlauer says that the war in Europe will end soon, and the one in the Pacific should wind up by Christmas. It'll be exciting to live in New York. Just think, you can visit us there."

Suddenly I felt homesick. "If I had to spend the rest of my life away from Puget Sound, I'd die a little."

"So would I, but we'll come home every July when the wild blackberries are ripe, and we'll show Bernard how to dig geoducks on a minus tide."

"And what do I tell your mother?"

Frannie laughed. "My parents will be relieved when I'm safely married off."

I helped Frannie find a dress, a frothy white creation with two dozen buttons down the front. I took pictures of this new and lovely Frannie.

Gone was the boy-crazy cousin who plastered her face with spit curls dipped in goo, chewed gum noisily and blew bubbles with it, and wore her cardigans with the buttons up the back so that her bosom showed.

After the wedding dinner at the Plaza Hotel and before the newlyweds departed for a dude ranch near Bandera, the Andlauers took me to the railway station. Just before I boarded the train Frannie tucked an envelope into my purse.

"There's enough in there to finance your first quarter at the U; small payment for all you've done for me."

Two days later as I sat in the railway station in Los Angeles, watching people squirm about like fish in a pail, I recalled the heady feeling of my first excursion away from home—the trip to San Antonio. I no longer felt the pulse of the nation and thrilled to the drama of people on the move. That magic was gone.

At the station in Sacramento, people talked excitedly and threw their hats in the air. Sailors burst into our car with the news that the war in Europe was over. One of them kissed me and called me "Honey." It was May 8, 1945, too late for Chris and Tadashi.

As the train mounted the four-mile bridge over the Columbia River, I rejoiced to see that Washington State looked as woodsy as ever, its blue-greenness blurred by a soft rain. As we flashed by Puget Sound, that inland sea between high mountains, I saw a curved pebbled beach, rimmed with huge bleached logs, each piling of an old dock topped by a blue heron.

The Mountain greeted me, majestic as ever, with a dark green ruffle around its neck. I responded as I did as a child: "Hi, you beautiful big old thing."

When I hopped off the train at King Street Station, the sidewalks were wet, but the sun shone and a double rainbow hung high in the sky over the City. If a building could be friendly and lovable, it was the Smith Tower, still the tallest west of the Mississippi.

Gina and Adrian were not at home, so I took the boardwalk to Nellie's place. I was surprised to find the door unlocked. Nellie had left a studio couch and a few dishes to tide me over. Suddenly I was overwhelmed with loneliness. I shut my eyes and summoned Tadashi. I wanted to hold his image in my mind forever, afraid it might gradually fade away like last night's dream remembered in the afternoon. My ears rang, and I imagined I heard him say: "Shikata ga nai, Robin. This is the way it has to be."

First of all I'd frame Tadashi's drawings and hang them on the wall. I'd buy flowers for the window boxes and a comfortable reading chair. Eventually I'd get a dog, one like Hanako, and a cat.

I dreaded seeing Mom and Dad, so I did everything else on my list except visit Grandpa and Grandma at Indianola. That could wait. I needed to call Aunt Vi to tell her about the wedding. When I finally did and apologized for taking so long, she exclaimed, "My goodness gracious, you precious girl! Don't worry your head about that." The lilt in her voice belied the disappointment I knew she felt because Frannie had not come home with me.

I went to the U, got signed up for fall quarter, and paid the $30 registration fee. Then I stopped at the Federal Building downtown to see if there were any part-time jobs available in Civil Service. As I entered by way of the revolving door, I came face to face with the Personnel Director. We recognized each other immediately, and he revolved himself back into the building.

"Aren't you the young lady I sent over to the War Labor Board? What are you doing now?" When I told him about my plans for school he paused a moment.

"I know of a summer job that might please you. It's with the State Department of Natural Resources. You'd be a lookout, or fire watcher, in a 12-by-12-foot cabin on the top of Mount Pugh, 7,000 feet up with a glacier 2,000 feet below. The rangers would keep you supplied with food. You'd have telephone connection to Darrington and a radio transmitter to keep you in touch with other lookouts. You'd have a front seat to Shuksan, Three Fingers, and White Horse, as well as Baker and Rainier. Are you interested?"

"Yes, please save that job for me."

"You're not afraid of being alone?"

"No, it will be an adventure."

"Come to my office in the morning and we'll set it up."

I felt so jubilant about the job that I decided this was a good time to see Mom and Dad, especially as I wore my best dress with white lace hat and gloves to match and my new spectator pumps. Mom would have to stretch things to find fault with my get-up.

After thousands of miles of countryside seen through train windows in the sixteen months I'd been away, I was happy to see some of the old landmarks on Yesler Way: the kosher market, the Chinese laundry, and Father Divine's Son Bill's Place.

As a bobbysoxer, I hated our old house with its steeple, but now I recognized it as a treasure. If Mom and Dad moved to Indianola as planned, who would climb the steep roof with the tar bucket to stopper the leaks?

I no longer had a key to the house, so I twisted the metal projection on the door that made a rasping sound inside. Dad swung the door open and he actually looked glad to see me. Even though he had never been a hugger-kisser, he embraced me and awkwardly patted my back, his hand flapping like a seal's flipper.

He pushed me into the living room where Mom sat at one end of the davenport and Uncle Fritz on the other. Mom froze with a long darning needle in one hand and scissors in the other. I kissed her briefly and shook hands with Uncle Fritz.

"Look at our little traveler," Mom said. "She's all fancied up. Are you home for good, or will you be traipsing off somewhere else soon?"

"I'm renting Nellie's houseboat."

Uncle Fritz whistled. "Down in that neck of the woods? Rough and tough, isn't it?"

"I like it. I can watch a parade of muskrats, otters, and Canada geese from my living room window."

"Violet says that Frannie married some ne'er-do-well Texan."

"Bernard's a concert pianist and he'll be joining the symphony in New York."

"Doesn't sound like the type Frannie'd go for. How come she got mixed up with the likes of him? I suppose you're here to pick up your stuff."

"Only my bicycle."

"You mean Chris' bicycle."

"No, my bicycle. I traded the bike he gave me for a Raleigh Gazelle." I knew I sounded angry so I tried to soften it. "I'll carry groceries in my saddlebags."

I remembered the small leather album in my purse; full of enlargements of favorite photos I'd taken in Texas. I fished it out and handed it to Dad.

He leafed through. "You took these yourself? They're good." He didn't add, for a girl.

Mom had rearranged the furniture, but the walls were the same, stippled in pink, lavender, and baby blue with sponges dipped in Calcimine. Chris had added splotches of dark green. I had always liked to imagine I was in a garden surrounded by lilac trees.

Mom picked a letter out of the wastebasket. "I suppose we should show you this." She handed it to me.

"Why are you throwing this away?" I cried after reading it.

"Because I'm not planning to answer her letter. They weren't married, so why should I?"

"Mom, they probably didn't have time to get married. Think how grueling it must have been for Chris to go on those raids and be shot at. She must have suffered plenty when he didn't come back. Aren't you curious to know what she can tell you about Chris?"

"No, I don't think she could tell me anything that I'd want to know." Mom had that cornered look she got when Uncle Fritz badgered her.

"And the baby? You'd give up on seeing your grandson, maybe the only grandchild you'll ever have? Are you crazy?"

"Your mother doesn't want to see her," Dad said. "She isn't the kind of girl we care to have in our family."

"Why are you ganging up on this poor girl? No one is condemning Chris. I'll bet she's a lovely person. Chris wouldn't have bothered with anyone who wasn't first-rate. She wants to come visit us, and you aren't going to invite her?"

Uncle Fritz stuck his oar in. "They are all alike. They want to find out if we are rich. She'll be sadly disappointed."

I felt the hairs on the back of my neck bristle. For years I'd wanted to beat him in an argument and bash him for his ethnic jokes. When I was little I'd been confused by this loving uncle who treated me like a princess and at the same time never let me forget that I was female and should aspire to nothing more than washing dishes.

"Uncle Fritz, you always talk about 'they' and 'them.' Who are these they-people you regard as scum of the earth? Did you read the newspaper this morning? Our GIs are going into those camps the Nazis built for the Jews. Now we know the awful truth. So you were wrong in thinking that stories about them were nothing but propaganda."

He surprised me with his silence. For once, he had nothing to say.

As for Mom and Dad, our differences were monumental. I didn't want to spend future holidays with them. Maybe I should disown them like Grandpa did with Rose and Pansy.

I handed the crumpled letter to Mom. "If you don't write to her, you may never hear from her again. Years from now you'll be sorry, and by then you'll have lost her address."

Mom... Dad... Uncle Fritz. They were hopeless, absolutely hopeless.

Suddenly Mom's faraway look changed focus. "You are right, Robin. You've got me curious to know what she's like. I'll write to her tonight."

Dad shifted his feet from one side of the hassock to the other. "I want to see that little guy," he said.

Mom was excited. She laid aside the scissors and the darning needle. Her eyes widened and she gasped a little. "This baby is a gift. Chris never knew that he'd be leaving us a wonderful gift. Maybe we can get her to stay in the States."

"Melody is her name, Mom. Stop referring to her as 'her' and 'she' now that we know Melody will be a member of our family."

Mom laughed and so did I.

When it was time to go, I skipped upstairs for a pair of tennis shoes. While in the basement, Dad extricated my bicycle from a pile of old lumber and brushed off the cobwebs. I watched him as he inflated the tires with the same pump he had used in the Twenties on the skinny tires of his Model T. Then he wheeled the bicycle out the basement door and leaned it against the house.

"What will you do with the car?" He pointed in the direction of the lean-to garage where Tadashi's Model A was stored.

"Don't worry about it, Dad. Kiko will pick it up when she gets back."

"I was sorry about him."

"Him? You mean Tadashi? Please, Dad, for my sake, call him by his name."

I must have looked pathetic pleading with him, ready to cry. What happened was remarkable. I saw my father's struggle between decency and prejudice. His mouth twitched. His magnified eyes behind the thick lenses darted back and forth as though he were looking for an escape. Then his face relaxed and he said with a modicum of relief: "I'm sorry, Robin, that Tadashi died."

I was too choked up to thank him. I squeezed his hand.

After riding my bike across town, I stopped at the top of the hill above the houseboats nestled along the east shore of Lake Union. I could remember when David Engstrom's codfish fleet spent winters moored nearby, sturdy ships with tall masts, gone forever.

The low-slung sun was poised to sink behind Queen Anne hill. On the lake a sailboat tossed in the wake of a tugboat and a floatplane landed nearby.

Six months ago, I had wanted to die.

Now, Nellie and I planned a bicycle trip. Gina and Adrian expected a baby. Kiko and Kenji would come home soon. Once the troops were transported, Melody and Little Chris could get passage on the Queen Mary. When Frannie and Bernard came in July, I would urge them to climb Mt. Pugh for a visit with me.

I was hungry. Maybe Gina would put on an extra plate, I thought, as I coasted down the hill.

Epilogue

I was lying on the beach at Indianola with a newspaper over my head, while my grandchildren played with little crabs much as Frannie and I used to do. They were talking about me.

Our children take us for granted, but it is sweetly rewarding when our grandchildren regard us as special.

I heard the little one say, "Did you know that Grandma was in love with a Japanese boy who got killed in the war?"

"I knew that," his older sister declared. "Did you know she spent a whole summer all alone on top of a mountain watching for fires?"

"That's nothing," interposed the eldest. "After the war was over, Grandma went to Europe to help rebuild youth hostels, and before she married Grandpa she made a trip to Japan on a tramp steamer."

"Wow," piped the little one. "Grandma is the spunkiest old lady I've ever known!"